BOWS, DOES & BUCKS

AN INTRODUCTION TO ARCHERY DEER HUNTING

MICHAEL A. DILORENZO

Illustrated by Jenniffer Julich

Adventures with JONNY ©

Running Moose Publications, Inc.
Clinton Township, Michigan

Published by
Running Moose Publications, Inc.
42400 Garfield Road
Clinton Township, MI 48038

Publisher's Cataloging-Publication Data
DiLorenzo, Michael A.

Bows, does and bucks : an introduction to archery deer hunting / Michael A. DiLorenzo. – Clinton Township, MI : Running Moose Publications, Inc., 2010.

p. ; cm.

ISBN13: 978-0-9777210-2-3

1. Deer hunting--North America. 2. Deer hunting—North America--Anecdotes. I. Title.

SK301 .D55 2010
799.277357—dc22   2009942505

Project coordination by Jenkins Group, Inc.
www.BookPublishing.com

Cover and interior illustrations by Jenniffer Julich
Layout and cover design by Eric Tufford
Interior photographs by Justin Maconochie

Printed in Canada by Friesens Corporation,
First Printing, January 2010

14 13 12 11 10 • 5 4 3 2 1

This Book Is Dedicated To:

Carmen Comaianni, who took me under his wing,
treated me like a son, and instilled the
passion of hunting deep into my soul.
For this, I am eternally grateful.

A special thanks goes out to all who helped with the creation of this book, including:

Jim Morrow, a.k.a. Bow Daddy, of MJC Archery in Clinton Township
and Royal Oak, Michigan, who steered me straight on archery shooting skills;

Tom Nelson, legendary bowman and host of *American Archer*,
who assisted on archery hunting skills;

Dave Richey, an outdoor writing legend, who assisted in archery
hunting skills and is a sounding board for my writing inquiries;

Bob Eastman, of Eastman Outdoors, for his support
and introduction to Lennie Rezmer;

Lennie Rezmer, executive vice president of Eastman Outdoors
and world-class archer, who assisted in field dressing techniques;

John Ozoga, retired DNR biologist, who assisted
with the section called "Interesting Whitetail Facts";

Justin Maconochie, multiple award-winning photographer,
whose talent turned basic hunting gear into eye-catching photos
within the book, without cracking one pun;

Jenniffer Julich, who once again brought the story to life with exceptional
illustrations as she has done throughout the Adventures with Jonny series;

NASP Contributors; and

my wife and family, who never let me leave without a smile
(perhaps I should be concerned!).

Last but not least, a very special thanks to "the other guys" who have gone on
endless scouting walks with me, set stands with me, hunted through all the worst
conditions that Mother Nature could muster with me, tracked and dragged deer
with me, celebrated or consoled over countless meals with me, and never, ever,
have let the conversations of past or future deer hunts grow cold.

Photo by Laura DiLorenzo

About the Author

Michael A. DiLorenzo (who really prefers Mike) is a married father of three residing in the outdoor-rich environs of the great state of Michigan. Mike has created the Adventures with Jonny series to entertain and educate children about the great outdoors and the adventures that eagerly await their participation. Knowing firsthand that a lifetime of awesome outdoor adventures begins with a simple introduction serves as his motivation to create and build upon the Adventures with Jonny series.

"If you give a child the gift of the outdoors, you give them a gift for life" are words that Mike lives by and came up with while on his own, in the middle of nowhere, doing what he loves to do most, simply being outdoors.

Look for all the *Adventures with Jonny* titles and the newest outdoor Jonny Gear on the *Adventures with Jonny* website at **www.adventureswithjonny.com**.

Adventures with Jonny, Let's Go Fishing!

Adventures with Jonny, Ice Fishing, The Coolest Sport on Earth!

Adventures with Jonny, Bows, Does and Bucks, An Introduction to Archery Deer Hunting

Table of Contents

Part 1

Jonny's Awesome Archery Adventure!

Building up to the Hunt – From the Sideline to the Frontline

Fall at last. It seemed as if it would never arrive. Now I understand why my father says this season should be nine months long. There has been so much anticipation waiting for my first archery hunt for whitetail deer. My deer hunting experience so far has been only that of a spectator. That changes this year when the bow will finally sit in my hands.

Ever since I can remember, I have joined my father in the autumn woods to sit as quietly and as still as possible alongside him in the deer blind. During our time in the woods, we have seen a lot of wildlife besides deer, including coyotes, squirrels, turkeys, otters, and all kinds of birds. We love it when the chickadees come out to play and flutter all around us, sometimes even landing on my dad's bow just to say a brief "hello" before zipping off to their next resting spot. The rapid fluttering of their wings so close to my head still makes me flinch a bit. Sometimes I feel like they are going to land on my nose or zoom me right in the face!

When my dad first took me out in the woods, we did not see very many animals. I couldn't sit still for very long, and I had questions about everything that I had to ask right then and there. My dad was patient enough to answer each and every one of my questions (as quietly as possible). Many times, they weren't even questions about hunting but rather about things I needed to know about life.

Over the years, I began to sit more quietly and I learned to hold my questions until after the hunt. That's when we started to see more animals. I remember seeing my first buck and how, even though he was small, I could tell there was something different about him as soon as he showed himself in the woods. I got so excited just seeing a buck that my heart beat faster and I shook with excitement. The thrill was like getting a great gift on Christmas morning, and that's when I began to understand why my dad spends so much time in the woods in the fall of the year.

This season, my role in the woods has changed from visitor to hunter. This year, I get to hold the bow in the blind. If all goes well and a deer comes my way, I get to shoot. I can't wait any longer. Thank goodness autumn has come.

Family Deer Hunting School – Bows, Blinds, and Bucks

This has been a very busy year for me in preparation for this hunting season. Since last year, Dad and I, along with my sister Kell, have spent endless hours in the back yard practicing our archery skills. Kell is older than me and has been hunting for a few years now and she is really good at shooting a bow. She has also taught me a lot of things that Dad taught her when she first started hunting.

In the spring, I took a hunter's safety class and learned a great deal about the proper handling of both a gun and a bow. A lot of the other kids in my class were just like me and were getting ready for their first hunt. We were all pretty excited when we talked about the upcoming season with our parents and the instructors.

Over the summer, we spent many nights with our friends coming over after supper to shoot bows until it got dark or the mosquitoes got too pesky, whichever came first. My dad told me over and over again that practice makes up for luck and how important it is to be able to shoot well all the time, not just some of the time.

Dad, Kell, and I also went on a lot of walks in the woods this year. As we hiked, Dad would tell us what the deer were going through or doing at that particular time of year. Our winter walks included talks about how deer survive the cold and the process of deer gathering together in heavy cover known as "deer yards" to stay warm. The spring walks taught us about fawns and when the antlers start to grow on the bucks. The bugs and the heat kept the summer walks to a minimum, but we still drove past farm fields at dusk to see the bucks in their heavy velvety antlers. Together, we spent a lot of time looking for good hunting

areas for both Kell and me to set up our bow hunting stands. We looked for tracks and old buck rubs, as well as bedding and feeding areas that deer would likely visit in the fall when we would be hunting.

My family has a piece of land in the north woods where we do most of our deer hunting. My dad and his friends, along with Kell and I, worked quite hard throughout the year to make food plots there for the deer. My dad calls the food plots "deer diners" since this is where the deer come to get some fast food. We planted foods that would be good for the deer to eat and that would still be around during hunting season when most of the other natural foods in the area would already be gone, things like brassica and winter peas.

It seems as if my dad has taken me through deer hunting school this year with all that he has taught me. Now it's time for my test.

My First Deer Camp – The Telling of Tall White Tales

Finally, the weekend came for Dad, Kell, and me to head to the north woods for what will be my first crack at whitetail deer hunting with my own bow and arrow. It's funny how during the summer months, we always say we are going Up North. But in the fall, even though we are headed to the same place, we are now going to deer camp.

We left right after school on a Friday afternoon, and Dad took this opportunity to review everything I had learned up to this point. Kell had plenty of her own advice to add, too. She put a tag on her first deer last season, and I will never forget how excited she was after that hunt. Dad and she arrived home as animated as if they had just won the lottery.

As Dad spoke, it seemed that for every point he had to make, he had a personal hunting experience to back it up, both good and bad. And if he missed anything, I was sure to get more advice from his hunting buddies who would be joining us at camp. I tried to mentally latch on to each of Dad's lessons in the hopes that I would do just as well or, on

the flip side, would not make the same mistakes he or his campmates had made in the past.

This was already becoming a much different trip for me since I was no longer just along for the ride. I sat in the truck with a fidgety stir in my gut, trying to imagine how this whole rookie hunt would play out.

In between stories and hunting lessons, Kell and I joked about one of us shooting a monster buck bigger than anything the other guys had taken in past archery seasons. Dad joked right back and said such an outcome probably would not get either one of us invited back to camp.

Our excitement grew with each passing mile. Although a few hours had already gone by, it didn't seem like much time had passed before our truck was turning off the pavement and onto the gravel road and we pulled up to the cabin. The inviting glow of lamplights could be seen from the windows and a cloud of smoke loomed above the cabin, fed from the chimney below. As I stepped outside the truck, cool air and the comforting smell of an evening fire welcomed me to the north woods.

Almost immediately the cabin door swung open to a raucous welcome from Uncle Keith and Mr. Mark that was surely loud enough to alert all the deer in the county that we had arrived for the hunt. Kell and I shouted back our "Hellos" as we struggled with our bags. We awkwardly walked into the cabin, fighting to stay on our feet as the weight of the bags pulled for the floor. We emptied the rest of our gear from the truck and closed the heavy wooden door behind us. I had just walked into my first official archery deer camp.

Our cabin reeks of all things deer hunting. For the most part, it's one big room with wood floors that greet wood walls and cause the smallest noise to echo around the room. There are a few worn couches around the fireplace and a frayed oval rug in between them. Right behind the couches sits our dining table in a small cooking area. A large bunkroom and a bathroom round out our cabin.

In between the deer heads on the wall are pictures of past hunts and lots of long nails that have been hastily pounded in with each dose of past nasty weather in order to hold wet hunting clothes. Now those same nails hold our coats and hats and the room is outlined with bow cases and boots along the bottom of the walls. A couple of old percolator coffee pots and a pan for the hot chocolate sit at the ready on the stove for the morning. There are short stacks of old hunting magazines wherever a flat spot exists, with curled pages that look as if they have spent many hours in the hands of the readers in the cabin.

The one thing about this cabin that stays with me the most is the smell of "old smoke" from the fireplace that fills your nose as soon as you're inside. I will always remember this smell and it stays with me every time I leave. To me, this is the coolest place on earth. (Where have you heard that before?)

As the echo of the closing door faded, Dad's friends started telling us about the deer they had seen around the cabin earlier that day. They too had lots of advice about going out on my first hunt as well as a story for every point they made, and their enthusiasm grew with each tale.

We sat around the fire for a spell, Kell and I completely entertained by the comical hunting chatter. Kell's favorite story surely was the reenactment of her success last season. We both laughed out loud as the supposed adults played out her reaction, hysterically imitating her excitement from last year.

After a late but delicious camp supper of homemade chili, we went to bed. A very early morning was waiting for us at the bottom of the clock, so we made our way to our bunks, quickly readied our clothes for the morning, and crawled into layers of checkered wool blankets.

Clearly, there were no rules that bunk time meant quiet time. The verbal hype rolled on only to be occasionally interrupted with a well-placed chili bean fart. Kell and I drifted

off to sleep with smiles on our faces to the sound of grown men laughing into the night.

Opening Day of Bow Season – The Wait Is Finally Over

A warm firm grip tightened on my shoulder as my father shook me from my sleep. "Why are you waking me, Dad?" I uttered in a fog. "I just fell asleep." In spite of my sleepiness, pretty soon the smell of coffee in the air (or was it the smell of Dad's long john outfit?) told me that morning had come.

It took but a moment for my eyes to adjust to the dim light of the bunkroom and take in the anxious activity of those in our camp. It was opening day, and my waiting had come to an end.

We heard the crash of the kitchen kettle hitting the table as the call for hot oatmeal sounded. A night's worth of sleep did nothing to slow the storytelling, which now flowed with unbridled enthusiasm. In between breaths came a continuing rundown of each hunter's personal checklist of what to take into the woods. I could only compare the exuberance of the adults in that tiny cabin to that of my sister and me on the last day of school.

The year's worth of anticipation was now an emotional dam break with this crew. These guys had waited for this day like I used to wait for my birthday. Despite the difference in years, they were as excited as little kids. Maybe, just maybe, you never really do grow up. I had never seen my father or his friends like this before. Opening day was really Christmas morning, October first!

After a quick breakfast, we pulled our camouflage hunting gear from scent-free bags. I paused for a moment, holding my hunting jacket to my face, and took a strong sniff of my clothes. This may sound odd, but scent-free clothes have a unique smell to them that always reminds me of being in the woods with my family. It is one of the great smells of the fall. I put on my jacket and we grabbed our bows and our backpacks and very quietly

left the cabin for our walk to our hunting blinds.

We walked out into crisp morning air, with an early frost coating the leaves that had already left their summer homes and covered the trail. The wind was calm and I could still smell the smoke of the evening fire hanging in the air around the cabin. Dad pointed to the sky with a big smile. Looking up, we could see through the clear north air a sky filled with more stars than I thought imaginable and a heavy moon sinking towards the horizon.

Dad whispered to me, "This is a perfect morning. Look at all those stars. This is what's so great about hunting. It's all the little things that you don't even think about that make it special. This is your first hunt, Jonny, and what a way to start the day!"

As we gazed up for a moment to take in the stars, as if on cue, a bright star shot across the sky, with a tail a mile long, and I couldn't help but wonder if it was a sign of good luck for me.

Uncle Keith and Mr. Mark headed off towards their hunting blinds, both to the south of the cabin. Dad, Kell, and I headed north to seek out our stands. Despite our best efforts, it was impossible to move quietly through the woods. Each and every footstep through the leaves on the ground generated a loud crunch that seemed to echo in the nearly silent woods. Nonetheless, the rhythm of our steps was hypnotic and lulled me into a trance as I focused on my dad's feet hitting the trail in front of me and the resounding noise that came with each step.

I was walking only a foot behind him when the woods around us exploded with noise. My father stopped so suddenly I walked right into him. I snapped out of my stupor and my heart raced with excitement. We had spooked a small group of deer and they ran wildly from the sound of our approach. We strained our eyes to see them in the dark woods, but we could only make out shadows as they dashed between the trees and quickly out of sight. The sound of their running stopped just as quickly as it had started as they tried to figure

out who or what we were. We waited a few minutes, and soon we heard them walking away in the distance at a not-so-alarmed pace.

We were nearly at Kell's hunting blind when this took place, so we knew we had to be extra quiet to avoid any more noise as we completed our early morning journey. In just a few more minutes, we reached Kell's blind. Kell tied her bow to the haul line hanging from her stand and silently climbed the ladder to her seat. She quickly attached her safety harness and pulled up her bow, giving us the thumbs up that she was okay and ready to go. As we walked away from her blind, Dad put out cover-up scent to disguise our presence and doe scent to hopefully attract a buck towards Kell's stand.

I took one more look back at Kell and saw that she was readying an arrow onto her bow. She must have known I was looking at her because she glanced up quickly, gave me one more quick thumbs up, and then appeared to be shooing me away so that the area around her blind would fall silent.

My First Chance – A Missed Opportunity

Dad and I continued our walk for just a few hundred more yards and came to a stop at the base of the tree that held our two-man hunting blind. The bow rope hung there in wait from our tree stand above. I tied my bow to the end of the line and we shimmied our way up the ladder. Once we reached the blind, Dad and I both attached our safety harnesses to the tree and then I bent over and hoisted up my bow. I slipped a broadhead-tipped arrow from my quiver and nocked it on my bow, relying on the soft sound of the click to assure me that the arrow was properly in place. Sitting back in the blind, Dad looked at me and gave me the thumbs up to make sure I was ready for this day. With all the confidence I could muster, I raised my own thumb and smiled. I was so ready to be here. Now the hunt would begin.

It would be dark for another thirty minutes or so, and I began to think harder about

what the morning held in store for me. Would I see a deer? Would I get a shot? Would I make a good shot? What else would we see out there?

I replayed all the things we had done up to this point – all the shooting practice and the scouting in the woods that had led us to this exact area, and how Dad and I had decided on this very tree for our blind. My mind was spinning with all things hunting.

But it was only quiet for a few minutes before the woods coughed up the first sounds of the morning. An owl hooted from a tree near our blind and soon another hooted in response from the direction of Kell's stand. There was dead silence in between hoots as one owl politely waited for the other's response. The two of them kept this up for several minutes, and I couldn't help but wonder what it was they were talking about.

Suddenly, the morning calm was shattered by the high-pitched cries of a not-so-distant pack of coyotes. There is a discomforting uneasiness that comes with the sound of banding coyotes when you sit in the midst of a darkened woods, but Dad assured me that I had nothing to worry about from the coyotes and urged me to enjoy the entertainment. The coyotes' tune, like the call of a loon, is one of nature's great songs that can never be played on an MP3 player.

Darkness had stubbornly held on to the morning, but now a skyward gaze offered a sight seldom seen by many: as the sun began to fight its way above one horizon, the moon was setting on the opposite side. Daylight slowly seeped in between the trees, and now the cast of woodland characters started to show itself. It was like the raising of the curtain at one of our school concerts or plays. Like the school warm-up band, the owls had now gone silent and a slow but growing melody of songbirds began warming up. They were soon joined by the start-and-stop rustle of leaves made by darting red squirrels in a state of constant chatter. Then the patterned cluck of a couple of black squirrels filled in the voids. Now came the raucous cackle of blue jays as they swooped to and from the ground in search of a morning meal.

Then my favorite little actors showed up, and Dad and I were greeted by the flit, flit, flitting of a band of chickadees that darted nervously around our blind. They landed but for a moment on the branches that enveloped our blind and one even boldly paid a brief visit to the end of my arrow. It often seemed that they were going to fly right into us, but they never did. The chickadees anxiously moved from tree to tree, and my eyes followed the loosely banded flock that eventually jittered out of sight.

Shooting light had finally come to the morning woods and a gentle breeze occasionally blew by, raining numerous brightly colored leaves to the forest floor around us. With each passing gust, this colorful shower filled the cool morning air. As I watched the leaves blow over our heads, I noticed a V-shaped formation of geese flying far off in the distance. Then the loud honking of closer flocks of geese could be heard and a couple of small gaggles of geese flew right over the treetops. Every once in a while, we heard what sounded like the wind of a small fighter jet flying by, whose noise came courtesy of small squadrons of ducks whizzing through the air so much faster than the geese. There was the occasional faint sound of gunfire from the lake some ways away, too. Duck hunters were out this morning as well, and were taking aim at the birds that had flown past our blind just moments before.

I was so involved in all that was going on around me that I was caught off guard when I saw a couple of does in the distant woods, easing their way towards our blind. I didn't expect the main actors to show up so quickly, but it seemed these deer were intent on coming our way. I glanced over at my dad to see if he too had spotted these deer and he gave me a reassuring look that told me he knew what was about to happen.

At first, I could only see two deer walking slowly between the trees, but soon a couple more showed up behind them. Dad and I had talked many times about what I might shoot that day and he'd left it up to me to decide if I wanted to shoot the first deer that came by or wait for a larger doe or even a buck. Just the sight of these deer had me so excited that I could feel my heart starting to hurry its beats. Soon the five deer were surrounding our tree and I decided to shoot the largest doe among them. They had no idea we were in the woods with them, and I felt very confident.

As I lifted the bow off my lap and began to tilt it upright, I grazed the seat of the blind with the bottom of it. Just this gentle tap made a noise that caught the attention of the deer like a morning alarm clock. All of them instantly zeroed in on our blind and I froze like a statue, but it was too late.

My stomach lurched as I realized what I'd done. In spite of all the things I'd tried to do right, I'd just done something so terribly wrong. It seemed as if all the other animals in the woods had fallen silent just for a moment and that my noise had clanged through the woods for all to hear.

The deer were instantly on high alert, stomping their front feet and bobbing their heads up and down, trying to figure out what we were. There was no calming them down. They stomped around for a few more moments, raised their tails, and then bounded out of sight, heading towards Kell's stand.

My heart sank. I was embarrassed to look up at my dad, but he leaned over and whispered in my ear, "It's okay. This is just your first hunt, not your last. There will be many more chances for you, Son. Just relax. The morning is young." This made me feel a little bit better, but I remained very upset with myself.

As the sun rose higher that morning, I could feel it slowly getting warmer, fading away the nervous chill that had come over me after I spooked the group of does. We waited silently, but besides the squirrels and birds, not much else showed up. I knew we wouldn't be in the blind much longer as there were chores we needed to do at camp that Dad wanted to get to before the evening hunt.

Soon my dad motioned for me to pull my arrow from the bowstring and place it into my quiver. This was his sign that the morning hunt had come to an end and it was time for the woods to rest. I couldn't help but think how much different the morning would have turned out if I had not made that noise. By now, I could have had my first deer. I was totally bummed out as I pulled the arrow from my bow and placed it in its quiver.

I lowered my bow from the stand and watched it sink towards the ground the way my emotions had earlier this morning. We undid our safety harnesses, climbed down the ladder, and began our walk towards Kell's stand. As we approached, Kell packed her gear, lowered her bow, and descended her tree, greeting us at the base of her stand.

We asked Kell about her morning hunt and she told us of a group of five deer that had run past her blind going a million miles an hour with their tails at full alert. I awkwardly told her that I had spooked those deer when I'd tried to lift my bow. I thought she would tease me for making the mistake, but she was pretty cool about it. Kell said she also saw a few deer way off in the distance, but could not figure out if they were bucks or does.

We met the other guys back at camp and relived our opening morning hunt. I let them know what had happened and they advised me not to worry about it. They both admitted to plenty of mistakes made during their early hunts, and reminded me that each one is a learning experience. "The biggest mistake you can make is to repeat your mistakes" was the message clearly coming my way.

11

As for the other guys, they had each seen a handful of deer and a couple of small bucks, but they both wanted to try for a larger buck so they'd let the small ones pass.

I was still feeling pretty bummed out about my mistake, but with perfect timing, Mr. Mark got that funny look on his face and proceeded to squeak out a very lengthy yet rhythmical chili bean fart that resulted in belly laughs from all of us.

All Quiet on the Hunting Front – Where Did Everybody Go?

The afternoon hunt produced not so much as a single deer sighting at our hunting coop. I spent that hunt determined not to repeat my mistake if I was lucky enough to get a second chance at a deer. I couldn't help but think that the morning's deer had told all the other deer to stay away from our stand and now the rest of the weekend would leave us without any other visitors.

Opening day came to a close with an empty buck pole next to our cabin and a sense of frustration in my belly. But once again, the evening chatter brought me to laughter and I began to understand that there is so much more to hunting than the kill itself. I did not merely see but could feel the bond that existed among the hunters in our camp; their common passion for hunting weaved their spirits together. I was thrilled to be part of this, and my personal frustration morphed back into determination as I looked forward to the next morning.

Unfortunately for me, the second day of the hunt began the way the first one finished, without so much as a fawn wandering our way. Kell was very tempted by a large doe that fed in front of her for some time, but she really wanted to hold out for a buck this season. Uncle Keith and Mr. Mark once again had the same small bucks show up at their spots, but they held fast in their pursuit of larger deer.

Slowly, the uneasy thought of going home empty-handed crept into my mind. We had but one evening hunt left before we had to head back home to the rigors of school and work, and I knew that at least a couple of weekends would pass before I would get my next crack at hunting. The chance of anyone's success this opening weekend rested in the final evening hunt. The adults did not seem too phased by this, as their experience had taught them that better hunting awaited them as the season matured, but I was just an anxious kid, and all I could think of was how badly I wanted to prove myself by bringing home my first deer.

The Evening Hunt – One Last Chance

Once again, the camp chore of splitting and stacking firewood for the long winter season ate up the midday rather quickly. This was followed by a bit of archery practice to keep us sharp and soon we were off to the blinds again. The weather on day two was the spitting image of opening day, remaining cool with the smell of autumn leaves hanging heavy in the air. The wind had picked up quite a bit and small bands of leaves rolled down the trail with each gust. The noise of the wind and rustling leaves overcame our steps and we were able to approach Kell's stand unnoticed by a doe and her two fawns who fed in the food plot below her blind. We stopped and watched them for a while, but soon the doe noticed our attendance and gathered her young and trotted away.

Kell walked off to her stand and we watched her climb in and get ready. Once we

got her thumbs up, Dad freshened up the scent and we headed off to our stand. We were settled in our blind for only a short time when we heard the heavy rustling of leaves coming in our direction. The noise was loud and sounded like it was being made by large animals, but it wasn't the sound deer made. At first we couldn't figure out what we were hearing, but soon a group of turkeys weaved between the trees in single file, following the first turkey like a drum major.

They darted their heads with each step and pecked at the ground once in a while looking for food. The noise of their march was occasionally drowned out by a couple of woodpeckers that had taken a liking to the dead trees in our area. They hammered out hollow tunes that were eaten up by the afternoon breeze. One rapid hammering drumbeat led to a fast response from the other, but not too often did we hear both of them pecking at the same time. How woodpeckers don't get headaches is something I'll never know!

The turkeys seemed very comfortable and spent much of the afternoon with us. As long as we didn't give away our position, I thought we would get the chance to see them roost for the evening, but this didn't happen. All at once, they began to get very nervous and an immediate heavy pounding in the leaves could be heard approaching from the area of Kell's stand. The turkeys didn't care to stick around and were gone before the noisemaker showed up. Despite the many falling leaves, most were still up in the trees, and the vale of leaves would not let us make out the culprit.

Our question was answered when a tall four-point buck trotted toward our stand. His tail was up slightly like he had been startled. After a couple of quiet hunts, I had thought the turkeys were going to be all that showed up this afternoon, but now it looked like I would have another chance, and this time at a buck. Dad signaled for me to get my bow up, quietly this time, as the buck made its way toward our blind. Instantly my heart raced, and I began to shake with excitement. Dad mouthed the words "Calm down," but this was a feeling I could not control.

The buck didn't look like he had any ideas about stopping, but without my knowing it, Dad had raised his grunt call to his mouth and let out one sharp grunt when the deer was within shooting range. The buck slammed on his brakes and came to full attention, his senses going crazy trying to figure out what he had just heard and where it had come from.

Double Buck Hunt – A Once Quiet Woods Erupts into Excitement

At first the buck looked right in our direction, but after a moment he turned his head and stared behind him. This was my chance to draw on him. I raised my bow in silence but it was harder than ever to pull back because I was so flush with excitement. I struggled under the tension of the bowstring and it seemed as if anxiety had weakened me. I finally came to full draw and settled my hand onto my cheek. At this moment, I could feel my heart pounding out a tune like that of the woodpeckers.

I focused on a single hair upon the buck's chest, paused for a moment, and released my arrow. I blinked when I shot and missed the path the arrow took, but the buck lurched at my release and jumped straight up in the air, then ran off over a small hill. By the length of his bounds, he didn't appear hurt, and I wasn't sure what to think.

"You got him!" Dad yelled in his loudest whisper. "You got him! You got him! You got him!"

I couldn't believe it. Now the shaking really started, and soon I was in an out-of-control, all-out body tremble. Dad grabbed me and gave me a bear hug that darned near squeezed the wind out of me. All I could say was "Thank you" to my dad over and over again. I had never thought I would feel like this.

It had all happened so fast I could hardly believe it had really happened. I'd made a noise on my first hunt, scared away the first deer, didn't see anything for two hunts, was

down on myself and frustrated at the very real possibility of going home empty-handed, and then boom, it all changed in a minute. I felt stunned.

Just as suddenly, we began to hear footsteps running in our direction. Could the buck I shot be running back our way, or was it yet another buck? In unison, we turned to see Kell bearing down on our blind in a full panicked sprint.

"I got a buck! I just got a buck!" she screamed in uncontrollable excitement. "There were two four-pointers that came by my blind and I got one! I just got one! The other ran away!"

"I just got the other one!" I yelped down to her.

My dad was in total disbelief at the sudden turn of events. Looking at him, you could see that he, too, was reeling with emotion.

I lowered my bow into Kell's waiting hands, Dad and I undid our safety harnesses, and we joined Kell on the ground. As soon as my feet hit the leaves, Kell wrapped her arms around me and we jumped up and down with excitement. My dad tried to calm us down, but he was just as excited as we were. The three of us were out there together in the middle of the woods, truly having the time of our lives. This was a moment I shall not soon forget.

Kell explained that the two bucks had been in front of her for a while. Every now and then they would spar and chase each other around the woods. She said at first she was very nervous, but then they were around her for so long that she finally settled down to enjoy the show, hoping to eventually get a shot. Finally, one chased the other right towards her blind. Their only interest was in themselves and they were clueless when Kell drew back her bow. When she released, the buck she shot fell to the ground and then got up and ran. She said she saw it fall again, not too far from her stand. The other one ran away, but she couldn't be sure in what direction it went since she was watching the buck she had shot.

Kell said she climbed down from the blind as quietly as she could and was just going

to walk over to get us. However, her excitement added speed to each and every step and soon she found herself in a dead run towards our blind.

Dad was confident that both Kell and I had made great shots on our bucks. However, he would not let us track either buck until at least thirty minutes had ticked by after each of our shots. The deer needed time to pass, and rushing our track could spook them into heavy cover or cause us to lose their trail altogether.

Just in case of emergency, the adults carried their cell phones while in the woods. Evidently, both of us getting a deer was an emergency, and Dad called Uncle Keith and Mr. Mark for help in getting our bucks before dark fell upon us and we had to head home. The two of them showed up in an instant, like combat troops ready for their assignment. They brought a celebratory charge with them that packed their high fives with arm-tearing energy. "Two bucks for two kids is an awesome archery opener!" blared Uncle Keith.

Once they joined us, we walked over to where I'd shot my buck and found my arrow sticking in the ground, a bright crimson coating covering the fletching on the arrow. We could also see several large drops of blood on the ground leading in the direction in which the buck had run. "It looks like you hit yours pretty good too, Jon," my dad stated with confidence.

Time was standing still for me, but Dad was carefully managing the whole event and now almost thirty minutes had gone by since my shot. He felt enough time had passed, so we began making our way towards my buck. Leading the way, Dad pointed out the spots of blood he was following, going right back into training mode. We made our way up one hill and started down the other side. About halfway down, Dad pointed to the base of the hill and yelled, "There he is!"

I was about to run past Dad to get to my buck, but he grabbed my arm and held me back. "We have to make sure he has passed before you grab him," he reminded me.

We quickly made it the rest of the way downhill and stood at my buck. When Dad could tell he had passed, he let go of my arm. I knelt down and grabbed the buck by his antlers and stared at my first deer. As I lifted his head and felt his now lifeless body, despite my excitement, I became so overwhelmed with emotion that a tear rolled down my cheek. Many thoughts ran through my head, but overall, I was just so excited and so thankful for getting my first deer and for having my family and friends with me to share this amazing experience.

Daylight was fading fast, and Mr. Mark suggested we drag the deer over to Kell's blind and gather her buck before dark. I tried to help drag my buck up the hill, but it was so heavy, I couldn't pull it but a couple of yards. Uncle Keith and Mr. Mark offered to drag it for me and we began making our way to Kell's buck, with her proudly leading the way.

Once we reached her blind, she pointed in the direction she'd last seen her deer. She guided us to where she'd shot her buck and her eyes quickly came to rest on her arrow. The scene was the same as mine, with her blood-soaked arrow confirming that she'd made a great hit.

"I think it's down right over there," she pointed. Dad and Kell followed the blood trail that vividly marked the way. In just a minute, they came upon her deer, lying right where she'd said it would be.

Dad checked the buck and flagged me to come join them. I ran up to Kell and high-fived her a bunch of times. I think we shoulder-slapped each other to the point of bruising. Uncle Keith and Mr. Mark were right behind me and laid my buck next to Kell's. They were darned near twins! Kell and I were on top of the world, and man did we feel like Mr. and Miss Big Stuff!

As happy as Kell and I were, it was our dad who was absolutely nuts with excitement. He muttered over and over his disbelief at what had just happened in what was not too long ago a quiet autumn woods.

In the fading light, we gathered for a quick picture before darkness put an end to a perfect hunting day. Kell and I grabbed hold of our bucks as Dad proudly put a knee to the ground between us and we beamed our smiles towards the camera.

Uncle Keith didn't have to say "Smile" for this picture. He pushed the button on the camera and sealed a memory that my family will cherish for a lifetime.

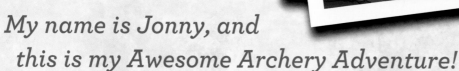
My name is Jonny, and this is my Awesome Archery Adventure!

Part 2

An Archery Hunting Tutorial

Introduction

Your travels through life will occasionally be steered by a life-changing event, something that has such a profound emotional impact that it imprints a lasting change in your course through life and alters who you are as a person. Throughout my early years, fishing consumed my every thought and the mere idea of using valuable free time for anything but fishing was a foreign concept. Then I went bow hunting and my life changed drastically. The culmination of emotions that were part of my initial bow hunting experience immediately addicted me to the sport. Since then, hunting and fishing have battled for my free time, with the autumn season finding more dirt under my feet than water. I have found the bow hunting experience to be one of the most fascinating and rewarding aspects of outdoor recreation, and I hope your introduction to the sport will place you afield for many autumn seasons to come.

The sport of bow hunting is actually a combination of two completely different skill sets, archery and hunting. You need to know and understand the basics of both archery and deer hunting before you can take to the woods in pursuit of game. But at some point, the skills that you learn in both arenas will marry together in successful unison and you will experience your first archery kill. This is a moment in time that will change your life forever. I warmly welcome you to the world of bow hunting.

Get Plenty of Vitamin H12

Although archery deer season lasts but a few short months, hunting is a way of life that can expand to other game, other seasons, and all twelve months of the year. Hunting is a physically and mentally demanding sport but it will provide great health benefits throughout your life. For one thing, it will serve as your escape when life makes you feel more like the hunted than the hunter. Hunting, at its most basic meaning, is the pursuit of something, be it game or a personal goal. Keep hunting for the good in life and let this good serve as your true hunting trophy. As the father of bow hunting, Fred Bear, stated many years ago, "It will cleanse the soul." No one had a cleaner soul than Mr. Bear based on how he made a life around bow hunting.

Keep yourself prepared for the hunt and for life by staying in top physical shape and by maintaining a positive mental attitude in all that you set out to do. Keep your mind and your archery skills sharp throughout the year by surrounding yourself with positive influences and continue to challenge yourself to improve in your shooting ability as well as in all else you put your mind to.

Share your hunting and all other outdoor adventures with others by inviting friends and family to join you on your excursions. Enjoy opening their eyes to the never-ending wonderment of nature and all that it has to offer. The kill is the finality of the hunt, but it is the hunt itself that calls us to the woods, compels us to rise early, pushes us when we are out of gas, and keeps discouragement at bay. Never stop hunting for what is important to you!

Archery Safety

The most common misconception relating to the sport of archery is that it is a dangerous sport. The thought of launching an arrow quickly brings images of people running around with arrows sticking out of them, shot by unsafe archers. This could not be further from the truth.

Studies have shown that the injury rate of kids participating in the sport of archery is less than one in one thousand participants. The same study showed that recreational sports like golf and fishing have injury rates that run one and a half to two times the injury rate of archery. Furthermore, the study also indicates that common, competitive sports such as baseball, basketball, and soccer have injury rates fifteen to twenty-five times higher than archery. The only sports listed as being safer than archery are bowling, badminton, and ping pong. But I bet if you dropped that bowling ball on your foot, it would hurt like crazy and drive up the bowling injury rate too.

All that being said, archery is only safe if you make it that way. Although you can shoot in archery teams or in organized programs, archery is an individual sport and only your highest level of personal responsibility can ensure that you and the people around you stay safe.

Since this is an archery/hunting book, there is no mistaking that the combination of a bow and arrow make for a lethal team of tools. Although the incident rate of accidental archery shootings is microscopic in nature, if all caution is cast to the wind, tragedy can occur without warning. Whether you are target shooting or hunting, you must always, always, always be sure that there is no one in the path or behind the target that you are shooting. Spectators or other archers must always be behind you or at the very least on the shooting line next to you. Never should anyone be even one step closer to the target than the shooter. Practicing this simple but very powerful rule will eliminate the potential for the most severe archery injury, an accidental shooting.

Most commonly, it is not the firing of the arrow that is cause of the greatest number of injuries. It is the mishandling of the archery equipment and most notably the arrows.

The bow itself has no sharp points, is relatively light in weight, and on its own is pretty harmless. However, the arrows are essentially pointed sticks, and anything with a sharp point, when mistreated, has the potential to cause injury.

In the sport of archery or when practicing for archery hunting, the arrow tip that is most commonly used is referred to as a field tip. The field tip resembles a pencil tip in that it has a sharp point but lacks any cutting edges. Nonetheless, since it does come to a point, it should be treated just like a sharp pencil. In other words, don't run with it and always hold the points downward in case of a fall.

Now then, there are two ends to the arrow. The end of the arrow that attaches to the bowstring is referred to as the nock end. The nock end of the arrow has a grooved plastic tip that allows itself to firmly attach to your bowstring. Though it is not sharp, the nock end is responsible for as many if not more accidents than the business end of the arrow.

The knucklehead zone is the area immediately in front of the target. Always make sure the knucklehead zone is clear of other archers before pulling your arrows from the target.

How can this be, you ask? Well, once the arrow has been shot into a target, there is only one way for it to come out and that is by pulling it out under force. When removing arrows from a target, the person removing the arrows must always check to make sure no one is standing in the direction in which the arrows will be removed. More importantly, you need to check to make sure no one's face is in this same area, say a person who is crouching down, looking intently at the arrows.

In other words, always look behind you before removing your arrows from the target to make sure you do not poke someone in the face or body when extracting an arrow. If you are in an archery competition, make sure all arrows have been scored and that no one wants one last quick look before you pull the arrows.

It may sound silly, but this is a realistic cause of minor injuries associated with the sport of archery. In a local archery club, I once heard an instructor refer to the area immediately in front of the archery target as the "knucklehead zone." The only person dumb enough to stand in this area would be a knucklehead. When looking at shot placement, or when you are removing arrows from a target, always stand to the side of the target and make sure the "knucklehead zone" is clear before pulling the arrows from the target.

When you have to transport arrows by foot, they are safest when tucked into the quiver of the bow or if they are in your hip quiver. If you must hold the target arrows while you are walking, grab the target arrows by making a fist around the field tips and be sure to hold the tips pointed towards the ground. By holding the arrows this way, in the event of a fall, it will be almost impossible for the arrows to turn around so that the field tip is pointing at you on your way down to the ground.

In Summary, Here Are Some Archery NEVERS:

Never aim your bow at an individual, period.

Never aim your bow at a pet to practice drawing on an animal.

Never shoot at a target if you are not sure what or who may be behind the target.

Never test a bow for sizing, fit, or poundage when it is loaded with an arrow.

Never dry fire a bow (fire a bow without an arrow), as it can erupt within your hands and cause serious injury.

Never spook, startle, interrupt, or sneak up on an archer who is shooting.

Never shoot at a target unless you have a 100% clear path to the target.

Never practice your archery skills where young children are playing in the immediate area.

Never, never, never give up (on a goal you are fully committed to obtaining).

(Advice courtesy of Winston Churchill during World War II)

Bow Hunting Safety

Once you embark upon your bow hunting adventure, there are two areas of safety concern, **woodland safety** and **hunting safety**.

Woodland Safety

Let's summarize what bad things can happen to you while you are in the field and what you can do to avoid or minimize the risk of each.

1. **Directional Hazard** (you could get lost)
2. **Injury Hazard** (you could fall and get hurt or cut yourself)
3. **Weather Hazard** (you could have to deal with sudden nasty weather)

Let's call these the Big 3 in field safety. Be prepared before you go into the field – bring a backpack that includes the necessary items to deal with the Big 3 safety issues.

1. Directional Hazard

a. Compass

b. Whistle

c. GPS

d. Cell phone or walkie talkie

e. Flashlight

2. Injury Hazard

a. First aid kit (band aids, Neosporin, aspirin, etc.)

b. Bottle of water

3. Weather Hazard

a. Rain jacket or emergency plastic parka

b. Extra layer for warmth (in cool climates)

c. Hot Hands (in cool climates)

d. Solar blanket (in cool climates)

e. Waterproof matches or other fire starter

Directional Hazard Getting Lost Stinks – Know your Directions

Before you take off on your hunting trip, make sure you leave a hunting plan with someone who is not going with you into the field that states exactly where you are hunting, the type of vehicle you took to the woods, your intended route, and what time you should be back. Set a "help time" with instructions that if you are not back or have not called by a pre-designated time, help should be sent to the area where you are hunting.

Directional safety items include a compass, whistle, GPS, cell phone or walkie talkie, and a flashlight.

First and foremost, if you're in the field, you have to have gotten there somehow. You need to be able to find your way both in and out of the area that you are hunting. You need to know directions (north, south, east, and west) and you need to have a compass with you just in case you get turned around. Prior to heading out on foot towards your hunting stand, take a compass bearing so you not only know what direction you are heading in when entering the woods, you also know what direction to go when heading out. Your exit route will be the opposite bearing of your entrance route. If you have a global positioning system (GPS) and are familiar with how to use it, bring it with you and make sure it has fresh batteries or is fully charged. Many of today's cell phones have a GPS system within the phones. Make sure you know how to use yours before you have to depend on it.

More than likely, you will be entering the field with your hunting mentor such as one of your parents or another older hunter who is familiar with the area you are hunting. That does not mean you simply follow that person like a lemming. Pay attention to landmarks near your departure location and landmarks along the way to and from your stand. Before you start your walk into the woods, look at your compass to determine the direction that you will be heading. By gaining knowledge about your direction of travel and the area landmarks, in time you will become familiar with the area and will gain confidence in your own travels. This comes with age and experience, and there is simply no need to strike out alone in the woods when you are just getting started.

If you are traveling to or from your blind in the dark, keep a flashlight on so that no other hunter in the area mistakes you for a big game animal. The best safety tip I can give a young outdoors kid is to stay with the mentor who brought you into the field. Until you are very comfortable with the surroundings, and this may take a few years, stay under their wing. If they are not hunting in the same stand as you, do not hesitate to ask them to take you to and pick you up from your hunting stand if you are not one hundred percent comfortable with finding your way. Getting lost is a very empty feeling and can be very dangerous. It is a risk not worth taking.

Despite wanting to dress in full camouflage, it's a good idea to keep a small hunter's orange vest in your pocket. In the event that you get lost or are in need of help, you will be much easier to locate by quickly donning the vest. Additionally, since bow hunting season oftentimes coincides with small game season in many states, wearing the vest while you travel in daylight hours will let other hunters know of your presence.

Whistle While You Hunt. Bring a whistle in the woods and discuss its use before heading to your stands. Have a plan so that everyone knows that the sound of the whistle is the call for immediate help. The internationally recognized distress signal is three evenly spaced sounds. The response to someone broadcasting the "three sound distress signal" is two evenly spaced sounds. Each person in the hunting party, even if it's only two people, should have a whistle on them at all times. A whistle can be heard at much greater distances than a voice and you can blow a whistle much longer than you can yell for help. If you get lost, or if you need immediate help for any reason, blow the whistle. Safety is more important than the hunt. If you need help, do not be concerned about bringing the hunt to an end for yourself or anyone in your hunting party. Blow the whistle.

A cell phone or walkie talkie is another great safety item that allows you to immediately contact other members in your hunting party should you become lost, injured, or ill.

If Lost, Don't Move. If you become turned around or lost while in the field, do not move. Stay where you are and blow your whistle. In most cases, the lost individual has not traveled all that far before getting lost. You will be found more quickly if you stay put than if you wander around and perhaps stray even further from safety.

Reassure Yourself. Your hunting mentor, friends, or family are not going to leave you alone in the woods. They will not leave the woods without you being with them. It may take a bit of time, but they will come looking for you. Tell yourself this repeatedly, as it is true.

Injury Hazard

The likelihood of a fall when traveling by foot through the woods can be significantly reduced if you take your time and watch your step along the way. Avoid walking on top of fallen logs as they can be very slippery and keep your eye on the trail for root systems or holes that could easily catch your foot and send you to the ground.

Be careful when handling your archery equipment, most notably the razor-sharp broadheads that are on the end of your arrows and your hunting knife. Use both of them only for their intended use and absolutely nothing else. Do not walk through the woods with your knife out of its sheath and do not walk through the woods with an arrow nocked on your bow, as both are recipes for serious hunter injury.

Weather Hazard

Depending on where you hunt or how late in the season it is, you may have to deal with sudden unexpected nasty weather. If it looks like the weather is about to turn very foul and bring heavy rain, lightning, snow, sleet, or strong winds, bring the hunt to an end and return during better weather. Depending on how deep in the woods you are hunting, it may take some foot travel time to get out. Keep a rain jacket in your backpack or an emergency plastic parka, or hunt with a waterproof jacket to keep your body dry. Wet clothes touching your skin will quickly draw heat out of your body and in a worst-case scenario cause hypothermia (a drop in body temperature). The rain jacket, an extra layer of clothes, and a hat and gloves can help prevent this.

Tree Stand Safety

Hunting from an elevated stand is a very productive way to hunt white-tailed deer, as you are above the sight line of a deer and you gain a scent advantage as well. However, once your feet leave the ground on the way up to an elevated stand, you place yourself at risk of falling. The only way to fully eliminate the risk of a fall is to stay on the ground.

If you are going to hunt from an elevated tree stand, you must follow every safety item listed below:

1. Select a safe tree, at least eight inches in diameter but not more than twenty-two inches in diameter.

2. Select a tree with a straight trunk free of other vegetation.

3. Use only TMA (Treestand Manufacturers Association) safety certified tree stands.

4. Always use a TMA safety certified full body safety harness and know exactly how to use it.

5. Always use the lineman's strap that comes with the full body safety harness any time you are in the tree but not safely in your stand and connected to the tree strap at your stand.

6. Always exercise extreme caution any time your feet leave the ground.

Injury safety items include a first aid kit with essentials such as band aids, Neosporin, aspirin, and water.

Weather safety items include a rain jacket or emergency parka, solar blanket, extra layer for warmth, Hot Hands, and waterproof matches or other fire starter.

7. Always be vigilant in your safety habits and be sure that others in your hunting party practice safe hunting as well.

8. Always have a means of contacting others in your hunting party in the case of an emergency such as a whistle, cell phone, or walkie talkie.

9. Always hunt with an adult or under adult supervision if you are under the age of eighteen years old.

10. Always follow the exact instructions for the use of your full body safety harness, climbing aids, and tree stand that were provided from the manufacturer.

Now that you know the things that you must always do to remain safe, here are things that you must never do when you are hunting from a tree stand.

Tree Stand NEVERS:

Never hunt from an elevated tree stand without the proper use of a TMA certified, well-fitting full body safety harness, also known as a fall arrest system (FAS).

Never attempt to climb or descend a tree with your bow, backpack, or anything else in your hands.

Never trust a tree limb as a safe footrest or climbing aid as it may look strong on the outside but be rotten inside.

Never continue to hunt from an elevated stand if you feel yourself getting sleepy, ill, or nauseous for any reason.

Never climb into an abandoned tree stand that you have found in the woods.

Never leave a stand in a tree from year to year as the growth of the tree can weaken the straps and integrity of the stand.

Never attempt to set up a tree stand in a dead, dying, or decaying tree.

Never hunt from a tree stand in foul weather such as heavy rain, lightning, sleet, snow, or high winds.

Never rush through your hunting preparations and make sure all of your safety straps are properly buckled before beginning your hunt.

The Proper Use of a Full Body Safety Harness

Before you even think about climbing a tree, make sure you have a TMA certified full body safety harness and that you know how to use it. To ensure the quality of the safety harness you are using, make sure it meets the Treestand Manufacturers Association (TMA) guidelines, which will be clearly indicated on the package. A good safety harness should evenly distribute your weight throughout your body, waist, and legs. Do not rely on the use of a single safety belt. These supposed safety systems of the past are actually not safe at all and pose a real threat of suffocation in the event of a fall.

There are essentially three components to a full body safety harness. First is the body harness itself, which is worn over your hunting clothes so that you can access the straps and buckles. Next comes the tree strap, which is wrapped around the trunk of the tree. Finally you have the lineman's strap, which is used any time you are in the tree but not safely strapped in your stand.

Depending upon the model of safety harness you have, some of the instructions may vary, but certain safe practices can be applied to every safety harness. These are as follows:

1. Read the instructions that come with the safety harness and become intimately familiar with how to use the safety harness you have purchased.

2. Inspect the safety harness to ensure the buckles are not cracked or the belts frayed.

3. Practice putting on the safety harness and adjusting its fit based on the clothing you will be wearing when you are hunting. This is key, as you will oftentimes be getting ready in the dark when heading out on morning hunts. It can be helpful to put small pieces of glow-in-the-dark tape on the buckles of the safety harness so that you can readily pick them out when hit with the beam of a flashlight.

4. The safety harness straps should not be so tight that they restrict your mobility and hinder your ability to safely climb the tree.

The use of a full body safety harness with a lineman's belt should be used any time you are climbing up or down from your elevated tree stand.

5. Be sure that all straps are properly connected through the buckles, are not twisted, and that enough of the strap is through the buckle so that it will not pull out (typically, this means at least six inches).

6. Practice using the entire safety system while you are standing on the ground so that you are very familiar with how to attach the tree strap to the tree and then to your safety harness. This is not something you want to learn when you are several feet off the ground.

7. Always run the tree strap around the trunk of the tree.

8. Never run the tree strap around a branch of the tree.

9. Never run the tree strap around your tree stand.

10. Never climb the tree or use a tree stand unless you have adult supervision if you are under the age of eighteen.

11. Never modify your harness other than strap adjustments as indicated by the manufacturer according to the safety instructions that came with the harness.

12. Have an escape plan ready, should you fall from your stand and be hanging from your safety harness. Know how to right yourself and safely return to your stand or descend to the ground.

Climbing the Tree

All TMA (Treestand Manufacturers Association) certified full body safety harnesses will come with a lineman's strap, which is a safety aid to be used when you are in the tree but not in your stand. Always use a lineman's strap when climbing or descending the tree, putting up a tree stand, or securing the climbing aids or ladder stand to a tree. A lineman's strap attaches to your full body safety harness and will keep you attached to the tree as you ascend or descend the tree. The use of the lineman's strap is especially important while you are setting

The use of a lineman's belt will keep you attached to the tree in the event of a fall during your climb. The lineman's belt should be used any time you are in the tree but not actually secured in your stand.

up your climbing aids since you will not have a safe, reliable footing source attached to the tree at this time.

Follow the exact instructions on the use of your lineman's strap that came with the full body safety harness you purchased. Each manufacturer will have slightly different directions based on the design of their harness.

Once the lineman's strap is properly attached to your full body safety harness, you will also need the tree strap that came with the safety harness to begin your climb. Again, practice with the lineman's strap and full body safety harness while you are on the ground. Once you are comfortable with its use and fully confident in your personal safety, you can begin your climb.

1. Wrap the lineman's strap around the trunk of the tree and through the adjuster buckle, allowing enough room in the strap to freely climb the tree or set up your climbing aids. Initially start with the lineman's strap around the tree at eye level and then continue to raise the strap as you climb the tree.

2. The lineman's strap can be used on all trees, including those that have limbs that you will have to climb past on the way up to your tree stand. Once you reach a limb, wrap the tree strap around the tree, above the limb that you have encountered. Run the tree strap through the tether on your safety harness and then through the adjuster buckle and pull tight.

3. Once the tree strap is secure, unwrap the lineman's strap from around the tree and raise it above the limb, securing it through the adjuster strap. Once the lineman's strap is securely in place, above the limb, remove the tree strap and continue your climb.

4. Once you have reached your tree stand, wrap the tree strap around the tree at shoulder level when you are sitting. The tree strap should have very little play in it once you are seated in your tree stand. If there is too much tension when you are sitting or it is very loose, adjust the tree strap accordingly.

5. Once you have found the right spot on the tree for the placement of your tree strap, mark the area with a reflective tack so that you immediately know where to place the tree strap the next time you arrive in your blind. Since your arrival will oftentimes be in the dark, the reflective tack will quickly guide your tree strap to the right spot.

The tree strap should be at shoulder height when you are positioned in the stand, allowing just enough room for you to comfortably make your shot.

The three point rule requires that you always keep three limbs in contact with the tree, which will greatly reduce your likelihood of a fall.

Climbing's Three Point Rule

Keep the "three point rule" in mind when climbing a tree. That is, always make sure you have three points of contact with the tree as you ascend or descend a tree. This could be two feet and one hand planted firmly on a climbing aid or two hands and one foot planted firmly on a climbing aid. The "three point rule" will significantly reduce the chances of a fall.

Bow Hunting Equipment: What You Need and What You Can Do Without

The sport of bow hunting is not immune to being diluted with many useless accessories that magazine ads say you "must have" but really don't need at all. I highly suggest keeping the sport as simple as possible in your early years and getting to know the equipment you do have as intimately as possible. Once you have your bow and arrows, the one thing you can add that will truly enhance the performance of your bow and your ensuing archery skills is practice, period. That said, the number one thing you need to get started in archery and eventually bow hunting is pretty straightforward: a well-fitting compound bow.

A Well-Fitting Compound Bow, Most Certainly a Necessity

A well-fitting compound bow is not just any bow off the shelf of any big box retailer. In order for you to shoot a bow accurately, it must fit you properly. The size of the bow, draw length, and poundage of the bow are all key elements that should be adapted to your physical size, strength, and shooting ability. Furthermore, the bow should be fitted according to your eye dominance, not to whether you are right- or left-handed. If you are left eye dominant, you should shoot a left-handed bow. If you are right eye dominant, you should shoot a right-handed bow.

The poundage of the bow is a measure of how many pounds of pressure it takes to draw back the bow. Many compound bows will allow you to adjust this poundage so that it can be increased as you grow and develop your archery skills. A compound bow with a draw weight of 25/40 means that it has a minimum draw weight of 25 pounds but can be incrementally increased to 40 pounds.

Modern compound bows can fire arrows at amazing speeds with very light poundage. You need to be able to draw the bow back without excess strain. If you have to point the bow to the sky to draw it back, this is way too much poundage for you and you will never be able to draw this same bow when you are cold or under the pressures of a hunting situation.

The draw length is based on your physical size and arm length. Most compound bows also allow you to adjust this as you grow by making adjustments on the cam or wheel of the bow. Not all bows allow the draw length of the bow to be adjusted, so make sure the one you are considering allows your future growth in the bow.

Compound bows have a wonderful little feature in them referred to as "let off." The let off feature reduces the amount of poundage you are holding when you are in a fully drawn position. The let off range of most compound bows is between 50% and 80%. What this means is, if you are shooting a bow with an 80% let off and the bow is set at 40 pounds, when the bow is drawn back, you are only holding onto 20% of the poundage or just 8 pounds of pressure.

The naked eye alone cannot distinguish the poundage of a bow, draw length, or let off, but you can determine all of this information by looking at the lower riser of a compound bow where manufacturers post a sticker that has information on all three key items and what they are for the bow you are holding in your hands.

Eye dominance, poundage, and draw length are the three things you need to consider when choosing the compound bow that is best for you.

The local archery pro shop is the best place to get properly fitted with a bow that fits your personal needs and allows for your future growth in the sport of archery. Having the proper bow is half the battle to shooting accurately and consistently.

I recommend a compound bow over any other style of bow sold today for the simple reason that it does not take a long time to become consistently accurate with modern compound bows. Unfortunately, in today's world, no one has an extra five minutes to put towards anything so keeping the learning curve to accuracy as short as possible is very important.

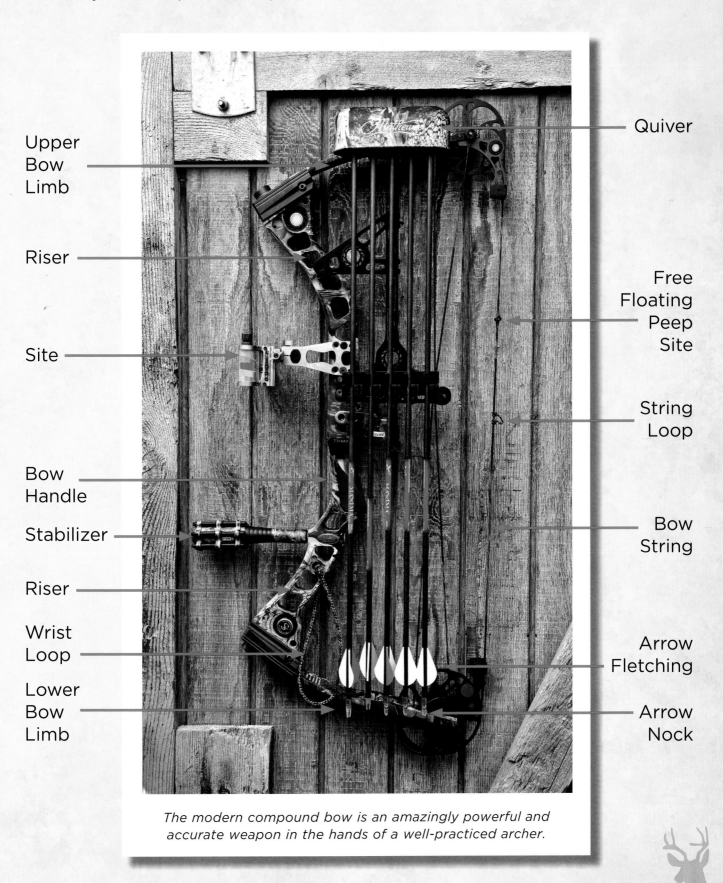

Upper Bow Limb

Riser

Site

Bow Handle

Stabilizer

Riser

Wrist Loop

Lower Bow Limb

Quiver

Free Floating Peep Site

String Loop

Bow String

Arrow Fletching

Arrow Nock

The modern compound bow is an amazingly powerful and accurate weapon in the hands of a well-practiced archer.

Arrows – Necessity

You really have just two choices in this category and that is what the arrow is made of, aluminum or carbon. Here is the key difference: aluminum bends and carbon does not. An aluminum arrow can get a slight bend in it and from that point forward it will no longer shoot accurately. A carbon arrow is much more rigid than an aluminum arrow and will not bend. A carbon arrow will either be broken or perfect. As a whole, carbon arrows are much more durable and should last considerably longer than aluminum arrows.

Regardless of whether you're shooting an aluminum or a carbon arrow, the arrow has to have the proper spine based on the poundage of the bow and the length of the arrow. The arrow spine is a measure of the stiffness of the arrow. In general, a bow with lower poundage will more accurately shoot an arrow with less spine (less stiffness). As bow poundage increases, the arrow should have more spine (more stiffness) to shoot accurately. The reason this is so important is that when a bow is fired, the arrow incurs a great amount of flexing as the sudden energy propels the arrow from a dead stop. This flexing is referred to as dynamic spine.

Most hunting arrows are made from aluminum or carbon. Typically, aluminum arrows are less expensive but have the tendency to bend, rendering them inaccurate. Carbon arrows are a little more expensive than aluminum but they will not bend and as a result provide a longer shooting life.

The length of the arrow also plays into the spine equation as well, but keep in mind that an extra inch or two on your arrow will not have that much of an effect at this stage of your archery game. If you start with a slightly longer arrow than is normally called for, as you grow and your draw length increases, you can still use the same arrows. Otherwise, if you purchase arrows that match your current draw length, once your draw length increases, the arrows will be too short for you to use.

Buying arrows is just like buying pants for kids. If they are a bit longer to start with, you can still wear them and grow into them so that you have them for a longer time without having to replace them. Arrows are expensive, so start with slightly longer arrows than normal (by a couple of inches) and you will get a lot more shots out of them.

A word of caution: don't fall in love with the paint job. You don't need an arrow with the most eye-catching camo paint. This may look cool in the store, but once you have taken a shot at an animal, it is darned hard to find on a leaf-covered forest floor.

I like arrows with an obnoxiously bright fletching and nock. These are the easiest to spot in the woods and I have never heard of a hunter being busted by a deer because of the color of his arrows, fletching, or nock. I find the most visible nock to be light bright green. This color nock is even more visible than any fluorescent colored nock.

The fletching is the group of vanes on the arrow that cause the arrow to spin during its flight and guide it accurately to its intended target. They are most commonly made from plastic and come in varying lengths. Some vanes are still made from turkey feathers, but I suggest sticking with the plastic vanes as they are more durable and there is not an appreciable difference in accuracy with either one. The length of the fletching is a matter of personal preference, and until you fire thousands of shots through your bow, you will not be able to notice any real difference between vane selection.

Ordinarily there are three vanes in each fletching, two of which are the same color. The odd color vane is referred to as the cock feather or vane. The purpose of the cock vane is to help the archer adjust the nock on the arrow so that it flies from the bow and the rest without coming into contact with either.

Field Tips – Necessity

Field tips could be nicknamed practice points. They are pointed tips that give the end of your arrow the appearance of a metal pencil. Field tips are used exclusively for practice and never for deer hunting. Field tips come in various diameters and weights depending on the diameter of the arrows you are shooting and the poundage of your bow. The weight of your field tips will have to match the weight of your broadheads.

Broadheads – Necessity

Broadheads could be nicknamed hunting tips. They are razor-bladed tips that are used for hunting. Make no mistake about it, broadheads are intended to be the "lethal" in the weapon. They are designed to bleed out prey as quickly as possible. Because of this, they need to be handled with extreme caution and should be inserted and screwed into your arrow only with the use of a broadhead wrench. Do not finger-tighten a broadhead, ever.

Here are two styles of field tips for archery practice and three different styles of cut on contact hunting broadheads, which extend the razor to the tip of the broadhead. The weight of your practice field tips and your broadhead should be the same.

Broadheads come in a variety of blade designs and shapes. The blades on a broadhead look like little wings and can have the same effect as a wing, which can cause them to fly differently than your fieldtip. As you prepare for hunting season, it is important that you practice shooting the broadheads that you will be using for hunting to ensure that you can shoot them as accurately as your fieldtips.

The most recommended broadhead for a starter archer is a cut on contact broadhead. Cut on contact broadheads are very effective, even with low poundage bows. The design of the cut on contact broadhead extends the razor blade right to the tip of the broadhead. Punch through broadheads have a sharply pointed tip, with the blades set about one quarter inch back from the tip. Punch through broadheads require a higher poundage bow and therefore should not be used until you can effectively and consistently draw a higher poundage bow.

The preferred weight of fieldtips and broadheads for starter archers, as well as many accomplished archers, is one hundred grains.

Sight – Necessity

The sight is an aiming device that helps you focus on your target. Nothing more, nothing less. Although there are many varieties of sights, the most common is a pin sight. A pin sight has multiple colored pins that can be adjusted for varying distances, as your bow will have to be held slightly higher or lower depending on the distance of the shot to your intended target. The pins can be set to help you hold your bow at the proper height for each given distance (i.e., ten yards, twenty yards, thirty yards, etc.). The sight is used as a reference point during the shot process, but it will always be the target that you will be focusing on, not the sight itself.

Peep Sight – Necessity

A peep sight is a small plastic aiming device with an open circle in the middle of it. The peep sight is placed within the strands of your bowstring. When the bow is drawn back, the peep sight allows you a clear view of the target that would otherwise be clouded by the bowstring. The peep sight also aids in consistent use of the same facial anchor point for your release hand.

Kisser Button – Helpful but Not an Absolute Necessity

The kisser button also attaches to the bowstring and is simply an aid to ensure your anchor point is the same every time your bow is drawn back. It is called such as the kisser button will rest in the corner of your mouth, just kissing your lips, when the bow is drawn back.

Silencers/String Muffs – Necessity

Think of your bowstring as a really powerful guitar string. When you pluck a guitar string, the vibration you cause creates sound. The same holds true for a bowstring, which in the world of hunting is not a good thing. Noise is the last thing you want when the bow is fired. Silencers and/or string muffs can be tied to the bowstring to absorb the vibration of the bowstring and bring silence to the bow, or at least make it a heck of a lot quieter.

Stabilizer – Not an Absolute Necessity

A stabilizer helps to balance your bow and absorb the shock that is created when the bow is fired. A stabilizer screws into the bottom of the riser, just below the handle. Target archers use incredibly long stabilizers that can be over three feet in length. Hunting stabilizers are relatively short in length so they are more practical to use in the field. A stabilizer does just what is says; it stabilizes your bow and helps to produce a more consistent archery shot.

Quiver – Necessity

Not only is this a feeling you will get when you see a nice deer in the field, it is also the name given to your arrow holder. The quiver attaches to the bow on the opposite side of where your sight window is located. The quiver also serves as a safety item for the hunter as the top of a quiver receives the broadhead-tipped arrow under a small umbrella-type cover. This shields you from having exposed razor heads while you are traversing on your hunt. Quivers typically hold four to six arrows. If you are a gun hunter as well, a quiver would serve as your ammunition clip, but remember, you only need one well-placed shot to be a truly effective hunter.

Release – Necessity

The release is a shooting aid that ensures a consistent release of your bowstring, shot after shot after shot. The release also aids in your ability to draw back your bow as it disperses tension throughout your wrist and forearm when you draw as opposed to having all the pressure on your fingertips when not using a release.

There are several different styles of releases. Most commonly, the release will have a nylon wrist strap attached to the release mechanism. The release mechanism itself will have a receiver that will hold your bowstring and some type of a trigger release. Try a few different styles to see which one feels the most comfortable for you.

The release is a shooting aid that allows consistent release of the bowstring for improved accuracy. The use of a release is essential on many compound bows as the short limbs create a pinch point at full draw that will not allow a hunter to shoot with a finger release.

Archery Targets – Helpful, but Use Only If You Have a Safe Place to Shoot

Unless you have a safe place to use an archery target, restrict your practice to an archery range at a local archery shop or sportsman's club. Regardless of where you live, if the backdrop to your archery target is another home, it is not safe to shoot at that target.

Archery skills should be practiced with both fieldtips and broadheads on your arrows. Keep in mind that some targets will only accept fieldtips, as they would be severely damaged by a broadhead or not allow a broadhead to be pulled from the target. This may require you to buy a second target that will accept broadheads. However, there are several good targets that will accept both fieldtips and broadheads, will stand up to thousands of shots from each, and should cost less than if you were to purchase two different targets.

Archery targets that accept both field tips and broadheads will reduce your need to buy multiple targets. Lifelike 3-D targets provide great simulation to a real hunting experience.

3-D targets provide the most realistic practice if your goal is indeed to become a bow hunter. 3-D targets exist that replicate virtually every game animal that walks the earth, allowing you to practice aiming at the kill spot of your intended prey. Watch for archery sales as 3-D targets can be pricey but will provide great practice. Also, virtually all 3-D targets will accept both fieldtips and broadheads.

Bow Case – Necessity

Bow cases are suitcases for your bow and your necessary archery equipment. A bow case organizes and protects your equipment when you are traveling to and from the woods. It is very important to protect your bow from being knocked around in your travels, as this can knock your sight out of whack and render your bow inaccurate.

You want to protect all parts of your bow when you are traveling, since damage to any part of the bow can have an effect on the accuracy of the bow. I prefer using a hard case, as this provides the highest level of protection for your bow and such cases have ample storage for all of your necessary shooting/hunting needs. The downside to hard bow cases is that they can be very bulky and difficult to pack in small vehicles.

It is imperative to be very organized when you are hunting. Keep all your necessary hunting gear packed with your bow, safely and comfortably within the bow case. This way, you will never arrive at the woods and suddenly realize that you forget your release, your arrows, or some other extremely valuable piece of equipment.

Binoculars – Not a Necessity

Binoculars are handy to have when you are scouting to see deer afar and learn their travel routes. While binoculars will also let you see deer off in the distance when you are hunting, they are not a necessity, as your effective kill range will be within twenty yards of your stand, at which point deer are readily identifiable.

Camouflage Clothes – Necessity

Camouflage clothes are a necessity if you are bow hunting or want to look outdoorsy in everyday life. Like the rest of the archery industry, camouflage clothing lines have grown. Today, you can find numerous camo patterns not only on clothes but on just about any piece of equipment that relates to the sport. You don't need camouflage clothes to participate in the sport of archery (although I think they look cool), but your personal concealment is key when you are archery hunting.

The three most important things you need to keep in mind when you consider purchasing camo clothing for hunting are as follows:

1. Think about the climate in which you will be hunting. What's the weather like? Do you need lightweight clothes for warm weather? Will it get much cooler as the hunting season continues so that you will need warmer clothes? What about rain or snow or wind?

2. What is the cover terrain of the area you will be hunting? (By this I most commonly mean the trees in your area.) Select a pattern that best fits with the background of where you will most likely be setting up your stand. You don't want desert camo if you are hunting in a conifer stand!

3. Is it functional or does it just look cool? There seem to be two extremes with youth clothing, either super tight or falling off. Neither work for hunting. Clothes that are too tight will not allow you to draw back your bow and will not allow for any undergarments to be worn in cooler weather scenarios. Likewise, clothes that are too loose will interfere with your shot.

Proper camouflage is a head-to-toe experience. However, it doesn't really matter if you wear camouflaged underwear. Remember, only the exterior layer need be camouflaged and do not overlook your hands, face, and head.

Regardless of what you purchase, make sure you try the clothes on at the store and go through the shooting motions. Does the jacket allow you to easily draw back your arms or does it pull too tight across your chest or cause the sleeves to ride up your arm? Will the jacket and pants allow for additional clothing to be worn underneath them? When you have decided on your clothes, make sure you shoot your bow while wearing them so you know if some part interferes with your shot and can be adjusted before you find yourself in a hunting situation.

My best clothing recommendation: purchase good quality wind or waterproof shells (jacket and pants) in a camo pattern that best suits your hunting location. Leave the camo shirts, socks, and underwear at the store as the deer will never see them.

The only layer that needs to be camouflage is your outer layer. If it is warm outside, just wear the shell over very light clothes, even shorts and a t-shirt. As the season progresses and the temperatures turn cold, pile on the necessary layers underneath your camo shell. You can wear neon green and electric blue clothes underneath your camo if you want, as no deer is going to see those either.

Most likely you will be hunting in an elevated stand without any cover from the elements, including rain, snow, and most importantly, wind. You are fully exposed. Even a gentle wind in cool weather can make you feel very cold if you are not dressed properly. Moisture in your clothes only adds to this problem. You have to be dry and "windless" to be warm.

Keep in mind that when you are sitting on your stand, you will be motionless and unable to generate any body heat. It is key that you dress properly to stay warm. Once you become cold, it is almost impossible to be still.

A camouflage hat, gloves, and a facemask are a good idea as well, although very dark colors for any of these items would work well too. Your skin is bright when compared to the often low-light conditions of the woods, so you need to keep it covered up as much as possible.

Good outdoor clothing is expensive, so try to buy it at the end of the season when stores are blowing this stuff out. Also, you're a kid and growing like a weed. Try to buy something big enough to last as many seasons as possible, but not too big that you can't shoot properly with it.

Scent-Free Clothes – Very Helpful but Not an Absolute Necessity

Controlling your scent is key when you are hunting, as the sense of smell is the deer's number one line of defense. Clothing that controls or eliminates your scent is very helpful, but it is also very expensive.

You can get away from spending this kind of money by washing all of your hunting clothes in scent-free detergent and sealing them in a plastic bag before you go hunting.

Even scent-free clothing must be handled this way to keep it as odor-free as possible.

Regardless of what you are going to use for hunting, it must be kept as odorless as possible or a deer will rarely, if ever, get within shooting distance of you.

Face Mask or Face Paint – Necessity

The art of total camouflage is not complete without addressing your face. A camouflage facemask will help provide total concealment when a deer has spotted you in your stand. Facemasks come in different patterns and different weights of material. If you are hunting in warm climates, be sure to get a lightweight mask and just the opposite for cooler or downright cold hunts.

If you are an eyeglass wearer (which I am), you may want to consider the use of face paint. Face paint eliminates the problem of foggy lenses when you begin to breathe heavily, which tends to happen when a deer is approaching your stand. If you prefer a facemask, try on several in the store and breathe heavily into them, imitating a high stress situation. Most facemasks channel our breath straight up towards our glasses, greatly reducing our vision at the most inopportune time. The fog-up factor will be further increased when you are in cooler or very humid weather conditions.

Although face paint can be the cause of some inconvenient clean-up post hunt, this can be minimized by using packaged moistened wipes when you come out of the woods. If you forget about having your face paint on and stop into a store or restaurant on the way home from your hunt, keep in mind that as much as face paint will conceal you in the woods, it has the exact opposite effect when worn in public!

Camouflage Gloves or Hunting Muff – Necessity in Cold Climates

If you are caught in a dead stare with a deer, you will want to have every inch of you concealed and this includes your hands. At the same time, if you are hunting in colder conditions, it is vital that you keep your hands warm so that you can properly draw and fire your bow. Numb hands will not allow the proper feel of the release and could cause a misfire when you least want that to happen.

The problem with many gloves is that they are too bulky to allow the shooter to feel the trigger release. The use of lightweight gloves will provide you with warmth and the ability to properly shoot your bow. Regardless of what glove you will be wearing while you are hunting, make sure you practice shooting your bow with your gloves on as you will more than likely have to adjust the wrist strap on your release to allow room for the glove material.

All shooting gloves should have some type of non-slip grip so that your bow does not slide in your hand when you are shooting.

Many hunters prefer their bare hands to be on the bow when they are shooting. If this is your preference as well, the use of a hand muff is essential. The hand muff will let you keep your hands together inside the muff and this "hand togetherness" greatly adds to keeping you warm and happy. Face paint could be used on the exterior of your hands to provide cover for those of you who wish to shoot bare handed.

The arm guard will not only prevent string burn, it will also keep poofy cold-weather gear from interfering with your bowstring.

Arm Guard – Not an Absolute Necessity

An arm guard serves the purpose of guarding your bow arm from the bowstring. If your forearm is rotated in towards the bow, upon release, the bowstring can give your arm quite a thrashing, commonly referred to as string burn. This can easily be avoided by using the proper grip when holding the bow. The proper grip will keep your forearm well away from the string and thus obviate the need for an arm guard. However, there may be a need for one when you are hunting in cold weather and you're wearing a "poofy," yes I said "poofy," winter hunting coat. The arm guard will hold down the material covering your forearm. This is key in a hunting situation, since your arrow will not fly where it should if your bowstring comes in contact with anything once it is released.

Rubber Boots – Highly Recommended but Not an Absolute Necessity

As I mentioned earlier, scent control is something hunters must address from head to toe. The boots that you wear into the woods should be free of household scent. If you wear your boots around the house and then into the woods, you are bringing every smell from your house into the woods with you, including your dog if you have one. This will do nothing to attract deer towards your stand.

Rubber boots are the best at controlling your scent as well as minimizing the amount of scent that they pick up. They are naturally waterproof and easily clean up after a day's hunt by just giving them a good dousing with a backyard hose. However, many rubber boots do not have much insulation value, so be sure to wear one heavy pair of wool socks if you are hunting in cooler climates.

Leather and nylon boots have a tendency to hold onto scent and are not preferred footwear when you are bow hunting. However, many of these boots are much warmer and more comfortable for walking and this is something to consider as well.

Regardless of your boot selection, try to avoid wearing them around the house (you should be taking them off at the door anyway) and wash the outside of the boot with a combination of water and baking soda to help get rid of any odors the boots have picked up. Just prior to entering the woods, spray your boots with scent eliminating spray, as this will help get rid of any odors your feet picked up along the way to your hunting location.

Backpack – a "Near Necessity"

You will need some type of a pack to hold your key hunting essentials. Many hunting clothes have oversized pockets that will allow you to carry most of these items. A backpack will keep your clothes from being weighed down with gear and allow you to bring a few creature comfort items like food and water. Make sure you wash your backpack in scent-free detergent as well. If you are using your school backpack, make sure it does not smell like last week's lunch or any cologne or body spray. Since this item will be with you when you hunt, a dark color or camo pattern is preferred. If bringing a backpack into the woods, do not wear the backpack while climbing the tree. Instead, attach a second haul line to your tree stand and haul your backpack up once you are in your stand and have attached your safety harness to the tree.

Knife – Necessity

It is always a treat to use your hunting knife, as this means success is upon you. You do not need a machete or a scalpel, but something in between. The blade should be approximately four inches long with a solid handle. Thin handles are hard to hold onto when you are in the cleaning process. If you are using a folding knife, make sure it locks into place when open. If it does not, it can fold down on your fingers when you are field-dressing the deer.

The backpack is your infield organization kit and should be home to all your essential hunting items so that they do not get left behind when you set off on your hunt.

No matter what type of knife you have, it is useless if it is not sharpened. Keep it sharp and keep it ready. You never know when you will need it.

Compass – Absolute Necessity

There are times when every tree, every hill, and every valley looks the same. A compass will always be there for you and you can believe what it says. Keep it away from large metal objects when you are using it and always check your direction when you head into the woods. The compass is as important as your bow.

Confidence in Yourself and Your Abilities – Absolute Necessity

Confidence is not an item you can buy off the shelves. You have to tell yourself that you can accomplish most anything that you truly put your mind to. If you sit in your stand with full confidence in yourself and your shooting skills, you will be successful at some point during your hunt. The more you practice your archery skills, the more confident you will be. This same rule will apply to everything else you do in life.

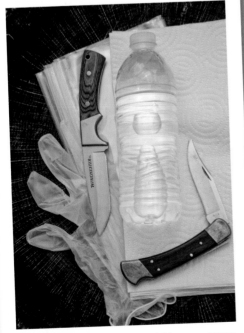

A good hunting knife should have a razor-sharp blade three and a half to four inches in length and a stout handle to provide a firm grip during field dressing duties.

Perseverance – Absolute Necessity

It may take some time before you bag your first deer. Do not get discouraged if it takes a few hunts or even a few seasons before this happens. Do not get too discouraged if you make a mistake that results in not getting a deer. Once you have set the goal for yourself to kill a deer with a bow and arrow, stay focused on this goal until you accomplish it. This does not mean skipping school and staying in your stand until you take a deer. This means putting forth your best effort every time out and practicing as much as you can so that you will be confident and ready when the time comes to take your deer. This also means not letting little setbacks deter your enthusiasm or keep you from accomplishing your goal.

Archery Deer License and Rulebook – Absolute Necessity

Once you have all your gear and you are confidently ready to hit the woods, you will need to have an archery deer license. The deer license is required in every state or province in which you will be hunting. Each state and province has different rules that apply to hunting and you will receive a copy of the hunting rules at the time you purchase your license. If you purchase your license online, there will be an electronic version of the rulebook for you to review. The license must be carried with you at all times when you are in the field hunting.

It is imperative that you attach your license kill tag to your deer as soon as it is recovered. This must be done before you begin to field dress or transfer your deer out of the woods. There are significant fines for not tagging your deer, even if you have a valid hunting license on you.

Read the regulations and be familiar with all that apply to you and the area in which you are hunting. Always follow the regulations and never intentionally ignore or disobey the rules set forth in the rulebook. If you are caught doing something illegal, the minimal punishment includes significant fines to you or your parents and loss of hunting privileges from one to three seasons or longer.

Ground Blind – Necessity If You Are Hunting from the Ground

The ground blind is used to provide concealment when you are hunting from the ground. Once again, make sure the camo pattern on the outside of the blind blends in with the landscape in which you will be hunting. Do not leave all of the concealment up to the blind itself. Location is the absolute most vital decision you need to make when using a ground blind so that you can use the natural landscape to truly conceal your blind. Depending on where you are hunting, there may be enough natural cover in the area to create your own ground blind out of fallen branches, fence rows, hay stacks, or ground vegetation. Be creative when putting together your ground blind. Think about what a deer would see if it were looking towards your ground blind. Would you blend in with the background or stand out like a sore thumb?

The ground blind can be used when the area you are hunting simply does not provide a safe tree in which to hang a tree stand. However, do not rely on the color of the blind material itself to work as your camouflage. Add further concealment to your ground blind by placing brush or small limbs on or around your blind.

Tree Stand – Necessity

In athletic sports, they say that you need to rise above your competition to be victorious. This can be said about archery hunting as well. Hunting from an elevated stand gives you many advantages including but not limited to your field of view, hiding your scent, and giving you the element of surprise. Any tree stand that you purchase should be safety certified by the Treestand Manufacturers Association (TMA). Depending on the location in which you are hunting, there are different stands for the job.

Check the regulations in your state or province to make sure the stand and tree steps you use are legal. Also, most states and provinces require the name of the stand owner to be clearly displayed on the stand. A permanent marker will do this just fine.

The Ladder Stand

The ladder stand is the safest type of tree stand you can use. The actual stand is at the top of the ladder. It allows the easiest access to your stand because you simply climb up the ladder and sit down. No monkey-type efforts needed here. Ladder stands come in one- and two-man stands.

The Hang-On Stand or Fixed Position Stand

The ladder stand and hang-on stand are two of the most practical and commonly used style of tree stands. They can be used together to create a great two-man hunting set up. This photo illustrates a twenty-foot ladder stand used in conjunction with a hang-on stand and how high it sits over a typical size deer.

The hang-on stand does just what it says – it hangs on to the side of a tree. Hang-on stands (also known as fixed position stands) can be as simple as providing a small plastic or metal seat with a small foot rest or they can be lavishly padded "easy chairs in the sky." Keep this in mind when selecting a tree stand – it has to be comfortable enough that you will sit still when you are in it. A small stand is light and easy to carry and is sufficient to do the job, and the tree will serve as your backrest.

The Climber Stand

Once again, the name says it all. The climber stand is actually a two-piece unit that allows you to climb the tree with the stand. Climber stands can only be used on perfectly straight, medium-sized trees that do not have any limbs protruding from their trunks. Because of this, they are hard to conceal and typically require you to travel much higher in the tree to avoid detection from the deer. Climbers can be difficult to use and can be rather noisy. I would not recommend a climber stand for a novice hunter.

Regardless of stand choice, look for a stand with a removable foam seat pad and take this seat pad with you when you are done hunting. It can be tucked under your jacket or placed in your backpack. Keep the foam seat pad odorless as well. If you leave it on your stand, it can get very wet and very chewed up depending on the weather and the animal residents in your hunting area. Take it from one who knows, hunting with a wet butt is no fun at all.

Tree Stand Lock – An Unfortunate Necessity

A tree stand lock will securely lock your stand to your tree. This is done not as a safety precaution but due to theft. Regardless of whether you set your stand on public or private land, a tree stand lock will ensure that your tree stand stays with your tree throughout the season and does not fall prey to an unethical hunter or passerby.

Climbing Aids – Necessity Only If You Are Using a Hang-On Tree Stand

Screw-in tree steps are a great compact climbing aid but are illegal to use on public land in many states. They can be difficult to screw into hardwood trees.

Climbing sticks set up quickly and with minimal effort. The climbing sticks closest to the ground can quietly be removed at the end of the day's hunt to keep unwanted guests from reaching your stand.

Tree Steps

Tree steps come in two different styles, screw-in or strap-on. When used properly, both work well and can be safe. Tree steps are used to help you climb up to your hang-on tree stand. You do not need these for a ladder stand or climber stand.

Always use tree steps as opposed to limbs when you are climbing a tree. Tree limbs can appear to be safe, but inside, could be rotten to the core. A tree step will never rot from the inside out.

However, most states do not allow the use of screw-in tree steps on state land. The concern is that the hole made by the step could damage or in some cases even kill the tree. Check with your state's regulations before purchasing your tree steps.

Strap-on tree steps are legal just about everywhere and cause no damage to the tree.

Climbing Sticks

A climbing stick is essentially a bar, two to three feet in length, with steps extending off the side of the bar. Climbing sticks are strapped to the tree and allow you to climb the tree with relative ease, much like climbing a ladder. Typically, three to four climbing sticks will get you to the right height for tree stand hunting.

Blind-Building Gear – Necessities You May Already Have around the House

The placement of a tree stand or ground blind will likely mean some modest tree trimming to open up a spot for your blind and to clear your shooting lanes. Remember to keep the landscape work to a minimum. A small limb saw or folding saw, hand axe, lopper, and a pole saw are all you need. You may only need one or two of these items at that. If you're thinking chain saw, you're thinking too much change in the woods.

Full Body Safety Harness – Absolute Necessity

No one ever starts the day by thinking to themselves, "Today, I am going to have an accident." Accidents are sudden and come without warning and only your thorough preparation will protect you or save your life in the event of the worst bow hunting accident, falling from an elevated tree stand.

If you do not have a TMA safety certified full body safety harness, then do not hunt from an elevated blind. Until you have purchased a safety harness and feel comfortable hunting from an elevated position, continue pursuing your game from the ground.

A limb saw or folding saw, hand axe, lopper, and pole saw are typically all you need to inconspicuously trim out your shooting lanes and provide access to your blind. Just remember, keep your pruning work to a minimum.

If you are hunting from a tree stand, the full body safety harness is the one piece of equipment that is actually more important than your bow. This is the piece of equipment that is most capable of saving your life, if you are prepared to use it properly, each and every time you go out hunting.

All tree stands that are sold today are required to include a safety harness. Unfortunately, the "included" harnesses can be difficult to use and are oftentimes worn incorrectly, potentially placing you at an even greater risk. Since manufacturers are required to include safety harnesses with their stands, they use the lowest cost alternative available to them.

There are much better alternatives that are much easier to use and that provide a significantly increased level of protection in the event of a fall. Simply put, the vest-style safety harness provides the best support around your torso in the event of a fall. Make sure to get a full-body safety harness with a five point safety system that secures your body, each arm, and each leg. Let's face it, you are much more apt to use a safety device that is not a pain in the

Next to your bow, the most important thing to take in the woods with you is your full body safety harness.

neck to get on and off. For all the money that is spent on the sport of bow hunting, do not scale back when it comes to your safety.

The full body safety harness must also have a suspension relief strap. This allows you to quickly relieve the pressure on your body and helps you regain your footing in the tree so that you can safely return to the ground. The suspension relief strap is a key life-saving component of your safety system. Without such a device, it may be difficult or impossible to return to the tree, putting you at severe risk of suspension trauma, which can be fatal in as little as five minutes.

If your full body safety harness does not have a suspension relief strap, you can modify your safety harness to include one by attaching a length of rope to the waist strap with a loop on the end that is large enough for you to fit your boot into, allowing you to relieve the pressure from the harness. The rope should be short enough that it allows you to "step up" into the relief strap and thus take your weight off the harness. If the section of rope is too long, it is of no value to you. Once you have securely attached the suspension relief rope to your vest, neatly wrap it up and secure it to the waist belt with a rubber band in a location you can easily reach in the event of a fall.

Prior to your bow hunting adventure, make sure that you have properly adjusted the safety harness to your body size, that you are comfortable with its use, and that you are prepared to get out of it in the event of a fall.

Although this is the last required piece of equipment, I want you to remember the safety harness first when you are assembling your archery gear.

Bow Hunting and Shooting Instructions

Eye Dominance

Before the first arrow flies from your fingertips, you must determine if you are left or right eye dominant. The human eyes do not come to focus completely in unison. Although you cannot detect this when both eyes are open, each of us has one eye that provides the dominant vision over our other eye. "Dominant" means which of your two eyes comes to focus first on an object.

It is your eye dominance that determines if you should shoot with a right-handed or left-handed bow rather than your physical strength or which arm you favor. If you are left-eye dominant, you should shoot a left-handed bow. If you are right-eye dominant, you should shoot a right-handed bow.

A left-handed bow is drawn with the left arm and thus the bowstring comes to rest on the left side of your face and is aimed primarily with the use of the left eye. A right-handed bow is drawn with the right arm and thus the bowstring comes to rest on the right side of your face and is aimed primarily with the use of the right eye.

Perhaps the biggest mistake people make as they enter the sport of archery is to shoot a bow that does not coincide with their eye dominance.

Testing for Eye Dominance

Either of the following two eye dominance tests will determine your dominant eye and thus the side of your body from which you should be shooting your bow.

Test 1: The Hand Triangle Test

a. Place your hands in front of you, at waist level, and form a small triangle between the thumb and index finger (pointer finger) of each hand.

b. Raise your arms straight out in front of you, keeping your hands together.

c. Now look through the triangle opening made in between your hands and focus on an object that is within six to ten feet in front of you.

d. Take turns closing each eye separately and see which eye remains on target and which eye comes off target. The dominant eye always stays on target.

Test 2: The Finger Point Test

a. With either arm, make a fist, leaving only your index finger sticking straight out.

b. Keeping your arm straight, raise your hand and point to an object within six to ten feet in front of you, so that the tip of your finger is blocking out or appears to be resting on the object.

c. Take turns closing each eye separately and see which eye remains on target and which eye comes off target. Again, the dominant eye will remain on target.

The Hand Triangle Test will allow you to focus on an object through the triangle in your hand. Take turns closing each eye, with the one that stays on target being your dominant eye.

Now that we have determined your dominant eye, the best course of action is to shoot a bow that coincides with your dominant eye. This will enable you to shoot with both eyes open, which is key for both safety and hunting factors as it allows you to maintain your peripheral view (side vision). In other words, keeping both eyes open enables you to see somebody or something that is entering your peripheral field of view. This could be someone who is about to accidentally walk into your shooting lane (safety) or a large buck that is walking in to spend some time with the doe that you have just drawn back on (hunting).

If for any reason you determine that you cannot shoot a bow that coincides with your dominant eye, you will have to close your dominant eye when shooting your bow. For example, if you are left eye dominant but are shooting a right-handed bow, once the bow is at full draw, you will have to close your dominant left eye and focus only with your right eye. In this case, if you kept both eyes open, it would be very difficult to keep your bow on target and shoot consistently well.

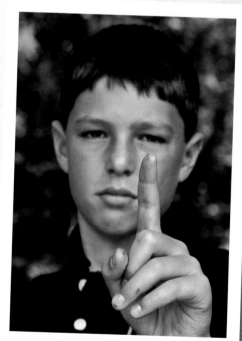

The Finger Point Test will enable you to point at an object. Take turns closing each eye. The one that keeps the finger on the target will be your dominant eye.

Proper Stance

Whether you are target shooting or hunting, the proper stance is the foundation for all else that goes on with your shot. If you are in a poor position, you can expect a poor shot. If you are in a strong solid shooting position, you can expect the same of your shooting performance.

When you are target shooting or standing while hunting, stand with your feet planted shoulder width apart, standing sideways to your target. Your bow arm should be facing your target. This stance will provide the greatest stability when shooting.

Maintain a straight up and down body position throughout the entire shot process. Avoid the surfer pose or surfer lean, where your body is angled in a rearward position. Other than looking cool, this does nothing for consistent shooting.

Your head should be held straight up and not cocked or leaned into your bow. This will set your head in a consistent position, which is also key to consistent shooting.

During a hunt, you may have to compromise the perfect shooting position, but if you maintain proper form as best you can, you will have a much better chance at consistent accuracy and bringing home your game.

This shooter illustrates the most common improper stance, the surfer pose where the archer leans back. Keep your feet shoulder width apart and your body straight up and down. Save the surfer pose for the water.

Holding the Bow

There is more to holding a bow than simply grabbing on to it and holding it for deer life (hah, in this book, that's funny) as you draw back your arrow. You will need to have a wrist strap or wrist sling so that you do not drop your bow at the point of release, as the proper grip is really not much of a grip at all.

Prior to placing the bow in your hands, take a look at the palm of the hand that will hold the bow. You will see an arcing line that starts at the base of your palm, in the middle of your wrist, and works its way up in an arc towards your index finger. This line is referred to as your lifeline. The handle grip of the bow should be placed just on the thumb-side of your lifeline, with your fingers gently curled onto the front of the bow handle but not wrapped all the way around the handle. If you wrap your fingers all the way around the handle, your palm will not be in the correct position to shoot.

The entirety of your palm should not be pushing on the bow as you prepare to shoot. Only the small area of your palm, between your lifeline and the base of your thumb, should be pushing on the bow. That's it. The proper grip will almost seem unnatural at first. Many archers report feeling as if they could drop the bow when using the proper grip. However, the pressure you apply on the bow when you are going through the shot process will firmly lock your bow into place. Once the shot is taken, the wrist sling will ensure that your bow stays with your hand.

The proper bow grip is not much of a grip at all. Hold the bow loosely with fingers curled on the front of the grip. The lifeline area of your palm should be pushing on the handle of the bow as you proceed through your draw.

The proper grip will also place your arm in the right position, so that it is has a slight bend away from the bow. This will eliminate the opportunity for the bowstring to come in contact with your forearm upon its release.

Up until you are actually ready to shoot your bow, you can simply grab onto the handle in any fashion. Once you prepare to shoot your bow, it is very important that you adjust your grip so that only that small area of your palm does all of the pushing and you have just a light finger curl on the front of the bow handle. Trying to choke the life out of the bow handle will only add to fatigue in your arm and help send your arrows in every direction but the one in which you want them to go.

Putting an Arrow on Your Bow

How your bow has been set up determines the exact location on the bow string where you must attach your arrow.

If you have a nock set on your arrow string, the arrow needs to be attached immediately below the nock set.

If you have a rope loop on your arrow string, the arrow needs to be attached within the rope loop.

Do not hold the arrow by the fletching when attaching the arrow to the bowstring, as you may damage the fletching. Instead, grasp the arrow a few inches in front of the fletching and then press the arrow onto the bowstring.

The arrow is properly attached to your bowstring only when you hear the faint click of the arrow locking onto the bowstring. If you do not push the arrow solidly onto the bowstring and there is no click, the arrow most likely will fall off the bow when it is drawn back. Or, the arrow may misfire once you release the string.

When attaching your arrow to the bowstring, hold the arrow by the shaft and press firmly onto the bowstring until you hear a faint click; this lets you know the arrow is securely in place.

Fletching Alignment

The position of your arrow fletching is dependent upon the arrow rest on your bow. The nocks can be twisted when the arrows are off the bowstring to properly align the fletching to match your rest design. Most arrows have three vanes that comprise the fletching, and one of these vanes can be a different color. The odd color vane is referred to as the cock feather or cock vane. This can help you adjust your nock according to your rest, but it is not an absolute necessity to have a cock vane on your arrow.

If you have a solid plastic flipper or plunger rest arm extending out of your bow window, the cock feather should be facing directly away from the bow window.

If you have a pass through rest on your bow, the cock feather should face directly downward so that it passes through the rest without coming into contact with any part of it.

If you have a drop away rest, the direction of the cock feather does not have any bearing on the flight path of the arrow, as the rest, which is so aptly named, drops away from the arrow.

If you have a biscuit-style bristle rest, the cock vane must face upward. The harder black bristles are your support for the arrow shaft, while the softer brown bristles allow the vanes of the fletching to pass with minimal resistance.

If you are not sure of the best arrow position for your arrow rest, hold the arrow up to the bowstring and imitate the flight path of the arrow as it would look coming right off the bowstring. This will give you an idea as to which way the cock feather should be facing to avoid any contact with the arrow rest on your bow.

Once you have determined how the fletching should be positioned, rotate the nock on each arrow so that all of your arrows will fly correctly and avoid contact with any part of your bow or arrow rest upon release of the bowstring. Do not simply twist each arrow on your bowstring, as this will cause unnecessary wear on the bowstring.

Bow Release to Bowstring, Come in, Please

The release aid should attach to your bowstring immediately below the arrow nock. If your bow has a rope string loop, the release aid should be attached to the rope string loop. Make sure your release is properly locked into place before drawing back your bow. Also, keep your finger away from the trigger until the bow is drawn back and is in the shooting position.

Pre-Shot Routine

Up to this point, everything you have read was a discussion of the "pre-shot routine." The pre-shot routine includes all the things you do that lead up to your shot. Be consistent in your pre-shot routine, as consistency throughout this whole process will add up to more consistent shooting. In summary, your pre-shot routine should be as follows:

1. Assume the proper archery stance.

2. Load an arrow onto your bow.

3. Attach your release onto the bow string.

4. Assume the proper grip on your bow handle.

5. **FOCUS, FOCUS, FOCUS** on the exact spot where you want your arrow to land.

Make sure your release is firmly attached to your string loop or the bowstring immediately below the arrow, keeping your finger away from the release throughout your draw.

FOCUS, Your Subconscious, and Your Trust in Both

You must keep both eyes open during the shot process. If you close one eye, the remaining eye will naturally focus on the pin and not the target. By closing one eye you will lose peripheral vision as well as depth perception. Keeping both eyes open will make you a much more accurate archer.

Before you draw back your bow, you must FOCUS on the exact spot on the target that you want your arrow to land. Don't think about just hitting the target. Pick a tiny spot within the target and lock both eyes onto it. Stare at it with the intensity of a mad dog. You must stay FOCUSed on this point throughout the entire shot process.

Focus

On

Connecting

yo**U**r

Shot

Staying FOCUSed on the exact spot where you want your arrow to land and not focusing on your sight is the ultimate key to shooting success. Keep this in mind: your arrow will land at the point that you looked last, all the time, one hundred percent of the time.

By staying FOCUSed on your target, your subconscious will bring your bow into position on the target and will tell you when to release. It will come as a surprise to you. You have to trust in your subconscious that this will happen each time.

The vast majority of archers have this the other way around. They focus on the sight and place the sight on the target, relying on their conscious minds to tell them to shoot after the sight is on the target. But as humans and not tripods, we cannot hold the bow perfectly still. Throughout the shot process, the sight is moving all over the target and when we think the sight is on target, we tell ourselves to punch the trigger. By the time we pull the trigger, the sight is coming back off target. The sight pin is always moving. The target does not move.

In a deer hunting situation, you are not going to focus on the deer's body, or the vital area behind the shoulder of the deer. You will be focusing on a single hair in the vital area, behind the shoulder, of a deer's body. That is what I am talking about when I say FOCUS.

If you FOCUS on the target, your subconscious mind will coordinate the shot as your bow is coming into position if you trust in it to do so. The sight will only be a reference point that you will be aware of, but you're not focused on the sight.

The key to shooting success is your ability to stay **FOCUS**ed on the target.

The intense FOCUS of the shot should find the archer glaring with both eyes at the target and his or her dominant eye peering through the peepsight.

Drawing Back the Bow

Stay FOCUSed on the target and do not look at your bow throughout the entire shot process. Raise your bow toward the target as you begin to draw back your bow. You should be pushing out with your bow arm with all the pressure from the bow on the little spot on your palm between your lifeline and thumb. Your release arm should be coming into position towards your anchor point.

If you need to lift your bow arm to draw back the bow, you are pulling too much weight. The bow should pull back without great effort. Too much strain will not allow you to shoot for very long and will greatly impede your accuracy. This will be compounded in a hunting situation when you are cold, nervous, or both.

At about three quarters draw, you will hit the valley of the compound bow, which is where the let off will kick in. The bow should fall into full draw at this point, requiring much less effort to hold in the drawn position.

Anchor Point

The anchor point has nothing to do with the last place you were out fishing on the lake. This is the area on your face that will become the hangout for your shooting hand. This is where your shooting hand and face will get to become good friends as they will spend much time together, in the same exact location, shot after shot after shot. The anchor point must be a consistent location at which your head can be

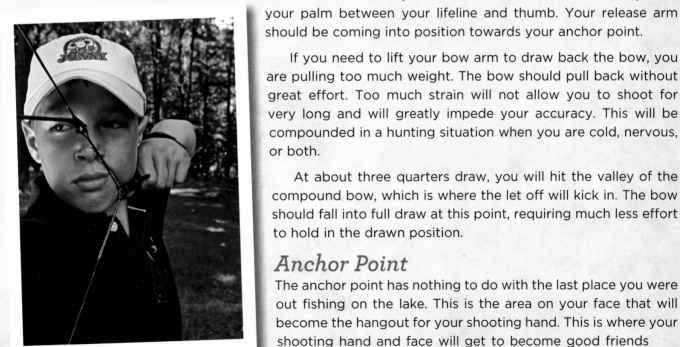

A consistent anchor point is crucial, as this serves as the launching pad for your arrow while you are FOCUSing on the target.

held straight up and you can easily aim your bow with your shooting eye comfortably aiming through the site and FOCUSing on the target downrange.

All shooters have their own personal preference as to the exact anchor point that feels best. Some releases allow the valley in between your index finger and thumb to lock into the bottom rear of your jawbone. See what feels right to you, but know this: the hand must be in the same anchor point on every shot you take in order to consistently shoot with pinpoint accuracy.

Taking Aim and Letting Go – the Release

It's never easy to say goodbye, but is sure is fun when you are saying it to your arrow.

Taking aim and releasing your arrow are so intertwined with each other that they need to be looked at and thought about almost as one single activity. Remember, you are aiming your bow by staying FOCUSed on the target, not on the sight pin.

The sight pin is an aiming reference and should appear over the target when you release your arrow. Zero in your sight pins by moving the sight pin in the same direction that your arrows are landing away from your target. If your arrows are hitting right of your intended target, move the sight pin to the right, causing you to move the bow toward the left to bring it on target. If you are shooting high, raise the sight pin, causing you to hold the bow lower to bring the arrow on target.

Once you have come to full draw and your hand is comfortably at your anchor point, now is the time to curl your index finger around the trigger of the release. The trigger should be in the first groove of your trigger finger, between the point of your finger and your knuckle. Curl your trigger finger around the trigger but do not apply pressure to try to fire the bow. This will happen on its own throughout the shot process. Never punch, slap at, or actually pull the trigger with your finger.

Curl your finger around the trigger of the release, once your hand has landed at its anchor point. Do not pull the trigger. Stay FOCUSed. The bow will fire as you push forward with your bow hand and pull back with your shooting arm.

It all comes together with this sequence of events. Once at full draw, with your finger curled around the trigger, stay FOCUSed with mad dog intensity on your intended target and more specifically at a tiny spot within the target. You should not be concentrating on your sight pin but burning your glare upon the target with the sight pin a secondary thought floating over your intended target. Slowly rotate the shoulder muscle (rhomboid) of your release arm backwards and push forward with your bow arm (with that little tiny palm spot). In your back, this will feel like you are trying to get your shoulder blades to touch each other. As you do this, the arrow will suddenly release from the bow when your subconscious tells you it's time to do so. The shot will actually surprise you and will cause you to blink.

In shooting this way, you do not pull the trigger with your finger. Instead, the tightening of the back muscles increases the pressure on the trigger until the bow fires.

The entire shot process should only take three to seven seconds from draw to release. If you stay drawn much longer than that, the bow will continue to travel around the target more and more. If you lose FOCUS on the target, let down the bow without shooting, gather your thoughts, and try again.

Shot Follow-Through

Once you have sent your arrow on its merry way, do not immediately drop the bow or your release hand. Keep both in place until your arrow hits its target, which happens in a split second.

Until that point in time, your bow should remain up and your release arm should remain raised at shoulder level. Once you have seen your arrow hit the target, you can relax your arms. This is known as shot follow-through. This is very important, as the natural tendency seems to be to get the shot over with so you can relax your muscles.

In anticipation of this relaxation, the arms begin to drop with the shot, sending your arrow off course. Think of this as your arrow being a plane and your bow being a runway. As the plane is coming up to speed and is about to take off from the ground, if the runway fell out from underneath it, the plane would not do so well. This is the same process your arrow is going through.

How Far and How Many

The definition of success in both archery and archery hunting is based on how accurately you can shoot, not how far you can shoot. Your goal is to become an extremely consistent shot with your bow, so that your learned muscle memory brings your shooting to machine-like automation.

Don't do this. This is not proper shot follow through. Dropping the bow immediately after the shot is the same as dropping a runway out from underneath a plane.

The best way to achieve this level of accuracy is to start target shooting at close distances and only extend your shooting distance once you are dead nuts accurate at the distance you are shooting. Your initial starting point should be no more than ten yards from the target and may even be as close as five. Once you are consistent at a given distance, increase your distances by no more than five yards at a crack to start. As your level of accuracy and shooting confidence grows at extended distances, make an occasional return to the shorter distances so that you maintain accuracy at all distances. You may become a great shot at twenty yards, only to have a deer show up within five yards and discover you forgot how to aim at such close proximities.

Tight groups of arrows that land on target indicate you have mastered shooting at a particular distance. By "tight," I mean arrows that are within an inch or less of each other. As a general rule of thumb, bring no more than three arrows to the line with you and once you have fired all three, look to see if there is a pattern as to where your arrows have landed. If you are off target, think about what needs to be done to correct it, make the necessary adjustments, and then fire away with your three arrows again. Three arrows will reveal if you are doing things right or wrong. If you bring a fistful of arrows with you to the line, some will group together and some will not, which won't teach you a darn thing about your shooting. If you have reached a good degree of accuracy, shooting a large number of arrows at once will result in damaged equipment, as some of them will begin to hit each other, breaking your nocks, tearing your fletching, or permanently damaging your arrows.

The two steps to proper shot follow-through are keeping the drawing arm raised and continuing to hold the bow up until the arrow reaches its destination.

Shot Summary

Putting all of this together with consistency shot after shot after shot will make you a tremendously accurate archer and a deadly hunter. So here it is altogether:

1. **Pre-Shot Routine**

   a. Assume proper stance

   b. Load your arrow

   c. Attach your release

   d. Assume proper grip

   e. FOCUS on target spot

2. **The Shot Process**

   a. Stay focused on target spot.

   b. Draw back your bow.

   c. Stay FOCUSed on target spot.

   d. Find your anchor point.

   e. Stay FOCUSed on target spot.

   f. Push bow arm forward and rotate release arm backward, until arrow releases.

   g. Follow through by staying in position until arrow reaches target spot.

   h. FOCUS on the great shot you just made.

You may have picked up on a theme here. FOCUS!

Change Things Up and Duplicate the Hunt

If you practice only one way, you will be prepared for only one shot. Vary the distances at which you practice your archery skills. Practice estimating distances between yourself and your target so that you know what it looks like to be either nine, seventeen, or twenty-two yards away from your target. You can practice yardage estimation by simply taking a walk, guessing how far things are from you, and then pacing out the distance between yourself and that target. Know how to adjust your shot based on varying distances to your target.

If you will be seated in your hunting blind, practice shooting from a seated position. If you will be hunting from a tree stand, practice shooting from an elevated position. If you will be seated in a tree stand, practice shooting seated from an elevated position. If you will be hunting in low light conditions, practice in low light conditions to make sure you can see your sight.

Go to a 3-D archery range and practice shooting at the kill zone on a 3-D archery deer target. This will give you the best practice in becoming familiar with how and where to take aim on a whitetail.

Practice as closely as you can to a real hunting situation.

National Archery in the Schools Program (NASP)

The National Archery in the Schools Program, commonly known as NASP, is a school-based archery program that is really hitting its target. The NASP is creating focused, disciplined kids with better academic grades, reduced absenteeism, and new social networks as a result of their participation in the program.

In March of 2002, Mr. Tom Bennett, who was then a commissioner for the Kentucky Department of Fish and Wildlife Resources (KDFWR) and Mr. Roy Grimes, who was then a deputy commissioner for KDFWR along with folks from Mathews Archery put the wheels in motion for a school-based archery program. The program was then introduced to 21 pilot middle schools and thus was the birth of NASP.

Rob Jellison is a seventh grade science teacher in the Hartland Consolidated School District in Hartland, Michigan. He is simply known as "Coach J" to his kids and is the NASP Coordinator for the school district. Since Coach J introduced NASP to the Hartland schools, over 1,200 kids have participated in just three short years. Coach J states, "One of the really great unexpected effects of the archery program has been its ability to break down barriers between cliques of kids with varying interests and social circles by putting students on the same playing field."

Both Mr. Bennett and Coach J, like many other teachers, have remarked at archery's ability to take kids of all shapes, sizes, genders, and athletic abilities or inabilities as well as many handicapped kids and bring them all together in one activity in which they each have the chance to excel.

Although NASP is a school-based program that typically is taught during school hours, many archery programs have blossomed into after-school events as well.

Through NASP, you can bring the great sport of archery to your school. The best way to get started is to ask your school principal to contact NASP through their website at www.nasparchery.com.

NASP can also be contacted at the following address and phone number:

National Archery in the Schools Program

2035 Riley Road

Sparta, WI 54656

Phone: 608.269.1779

Fax: 608.269.0172

For starters, hunt for a good mentor before you hunt for deer. After you've done this, learn as much as you can about the animal itself. In my opinion, you should learn about the deer before you learn about deer hunting. Books written by well-respected deer biologists such as John Ozoga or Leonard Lee Rue III will teach you about the entire life cycle of a deer. Once you know its needs (deer do not have wants) and behavior patterns, you will know where to find them on any piece of property that you hunt as well as how to hunt them.

Deer hunting magazines tend to focus on deer hunting techniques and to a lesser degree on deer behavior. Once you have the basic knowledge of why a deer does what it does, you will know how to apply various hunting techniques and they will make more sense to you. The written biological facts will help you gain a genuine understanding of the life cycle of deer from birth through their youth and into their adulthood. Learn about their life-sustaining needs and where the best location is to find them in their daily job of survival.

Most hunting videos, while entertaining, don't do a lot for improving your knowledge about white-tailed deer. Typically, hunting videos focus on taking trophy size animals by professional archers, oftentimes in controlled environments. They set an unrealistic level of expectation for the novice hunter. As far as I'm concerned, any deer that you take with a bow in your early years of hunting is a trophy.

By the way, playing a video game about hunting doesn't do much to add to your knowledge base about white-tailed deer, either. Far and away the best way to learn about deer hunting is to spend time with a good hunting mentor such as a parent, grandparent, aunt or uncle, close neighbor, or family friend who is serious about the sport of archery deer hunting. I find that most serious archery hunters are also serious about teaching the sport to the younger generation and will happily take you under their wing to help your entry into the sport. Talking with folks who have spent a great deal of time in the woods will provide the best education in the do's and don'ts of deer hunting. Anyone who has actively pursued deer has made mistakes and learned from them and can prevent you from making the same mistakes if you openly listen to what they have to say and practice what they preach.

You can also learn an awful lot about deer hunting by talking with unsuccessful hunters. Listen closely to what they have done during their hunts, especially the things that made them unsuccessful (which they will not willingly cough up), and then don't do those things.

Pay close attention when talking with your mentors, as what they tell you may not come in the form of a specific lesson but rather will be what you glean from the hunting stories you are told. Listen to what worked on their successful hunts and what they did on other hunts that did not work out so well. There will be times when they may specifically tell you what to do or how to do it, but there is also vast knowledge and entertainment in letting them share their past hunting experiences with you, so keep your ears open.

Time is why deer and deer hunting education is so important, or more specifically, the lack of it. Deer season only comes once a year and only lasts for so many days, which varies by each state or province. Of the entirety of the deer season, you can only hunt so many of those days. Each of those days out hunting is a precious window of opportunity. You can either take a great knowledge base into the woods with you and significantly speed up your road to success or go out armed only with your bow and be forced to rely on freakishly good luck for your success and at the same time extend by years the time it takes to learn how to do things right.

Know What You Are Up Against

The only thing on a deer's mind every waking minute is survival. This survival has three basic components, what I call "the Three S's": sustenance (food and water), shelter, and species continuation. Deer are always thinking about where their next meal is coming from, what good cover is in the area to provide them with a safe haven from predators or the elements, and in the fall of the year, deer dating.

The whitetail is a crepuscular ruminant. (That's pretty fancy talk isn't it?) The crepuscular part means they favor low light conditions such as early morning, just after dark, or early evening, just before dark. The ruminant part means they have a chambered stomach, which allows them to quickly take down large amounts of food and store it in their stomachs to be coughed up later and chewed more thoroughly.

So what does their being a crepuscular ruminant mean to you? Well, first of all, most of you just learned two new words. Second, it means you need to be in your stand hunting these deer during the day's low light conditions that deer prefer. This means being in your stand early, before the low light conditions prevail on the morning hunts, and that you stay in your stand throughout the low light conditions in the evening, until darkness falls upon the woods on the evening hunts. Third, this information should tell you that deer are not going to spend a lot of time feeding in one particular area (feeding spot), as they are going to settle down where they feel comfortable after eating and begin chewing on the food they recently ate before maybe catching some z's (bedding spot).

As a hunter, you need to find these feeding and bedding spots and set your stands near them or on the trails that connect the two together. That's something else you may not know. For the most part, deer do not wander aimlessly throughout the woods. Rather, they use well-established deer trails to travel to and from their feeding and bedding spots. Pay close attention to ground vegetation and the ground itself where you are hunting and look for a narrow trampled path that weaves through field grasses or deer prints. If you look closely enough at the path, specifically where the ground is exposed on the path, you should be able to identify hoof prints from the deer to confirm that it is indeed a deer trail.

Think about each fact you learn about deer and how you can improve your hunting skills by adding that new-found bit of information to your ever-growing knowledge base.

Deer Food

Deer have ravenous appetites that are fed by a wide variety of plant life. The native fauna or crop of choice will vary depending on the geographic location of the deer and the season. Deer are herbivores, so you need not worry about any man-eating bucks while out hunting.

On the crop menu, corn, apples, carrots, potatoes (raw, not fried, and no butter, sour cream, or ketchup is necessary), and soybeans are among deer's preferred foods, though there are many other crop items that deer will happily feed upon.

On the native plant menu, deer are wild about acorns (especially from white oaks), clover, lush grasses such as rye, blueberries, locust seed pods, sumac, and so many others.

Deer are not easily swayed by junk food. They will look to eat the most nutritious food in the area first and then work their way down the nutrition chart as they exhaust the best foods or these foods become unavailable due to regional climatic conditions.

On private land, the use of food plots is a highly effective way to draw deer to your stand and to keep deer in your area. A food plot will become a natural food source for the deer that can draw deer to your hunting land throughout the year. A food plot is just that, a small plot of land that is cleared of natural growth and planted with any of a number of a deer's favorite foods, including but not limited to rye, clover, brassica, winter peas, sugar beets, etc. Food plots should still be developed in an area that provides good natural cover for deer, limiting the amount of travel it takes the deer to reach your plot. A food plot takes some effort to establish, but it is an enjoyable task to work the land and reap the rewards of seeing the deer drawn to your efforts. The entire food plot will not be within your EFFECTIVE KILL RANGE, so set your stand near a primary deer trail entering or exiting the food plot.

Deer baiting is the act of bringing deer food in the woods to your hunting location and setting it out for the deer to eat within your EFFECTIVE KILL RANGE. This method of attracting deer can be highly effective but can also alter a deer's natural feeding pattern, sending a lot of deer to your bait during the nighttime hours as they become suspicious about the random food offering. Natural deer bait includes corn, apples, beets, and carrots. There are also manufactured deer baits including mineral blocks, salt blocks, treated corn, syrups, and powders that are mixed with water and poured into the ground. Deer baiting is not legal in all states and those states that do allow deer baiting often specify what bait is legal to use, establish limits as to how much food you can set out in the woods, and establish time frame (seasonal) limits. Refer to your state or province's hunting rulebook before you begin to bait deer.

Where to Find Them – Scouting

The act of scouting occurs every time you are in the woods. Keeping a vigilant eye for deer sign, feeding areas, bedding areas, and sanctuaries will help you better understand the patterns of white-tailed deer and will constantly increase your knowledge base, which will pay great dividends when it comes to your deer hunting success.

Scouting can be done all year round. It is a great family activity that in large part involves quiet walks in the woods, observing nature, and looking for clues that will lead you and other members of your hunting party to a successful archery season.

Many hunters will tell you that if you find the food, you will find the deer. This is true in many cases. However, deer must have shelter in close proximity to their feeding area. Shelter to a deer is normally very heavy thick vegetation or tree growth that you as a person will not want to walk into or that you may have to get on your hands and knees to traverse. When deer are not feeding, they will bed down within this thick growth. It is their sanctuary. You are best to leave it at that, and once you locate the thick cover, not enter it. If you do enter it, more often than not, deer will feel as if they have been discovered and will find another sanctuary. When you enter their sanctuary, you enter their home. If the roles were reversed and an unwanted visitor entered your home, you would be very nervous about re-entering your own home again.

Generally, the thickest growth in a specific area is the comfort zone for deer. An area that provides them with the ability to disappear from imminent danger, such as man, is vital to their comfort and survival. Do not underestimate a deer's ability (even a large buck) to quickly disappear into an area that you thought no large creature could ever enter, let alone call their home.

So let's paint this picture...

If you found a bean field where you regularly saw deer and next to the bean field was a stand of wide open hardwoods and not too far within those hardwoods was a very thick tangled stand of cedar trees, the area between the bean field and the cedar swamp would be a great place to set up your stand. Specifically, you would want to pay close attention to the ground in order to set your stand within your EFFECTIVE KILL RANGE of the most heavily used deer trail running between the bean field and the cedar swamp.

If all you had was a giant bean field and this was bordered by yet another low growing field and then another, you might not have much opportunity to find deer despite the abundance of food in the area. In this case, deer might be using the cover of darkness as their shelter and feeding in those areas only at night.

Deer tracks vary in size, not just by the weight of the deer but also the softness of the ground. A track with crisp edges is fresh off the hoof. Older tracks will lack sharp edge detail.

Woodlands have plenty of food to offer deer as well and the location of these food sources is another good place to find deer. Learn about the preferred woodland foods in the area that you are hunting and how to readily identify such trees or plants. Locate these food sources, keep the thought of nearby sanctuary in mind, and then determine the best area for your stand.

We've chatted about food and shelter, but the other half of sustenance is water. Having a good water source near your hunting location will add to your chances of success, since water is vital to deers' survival. If you are hunting in the upper Midwest area of the country, water is extremely abundant and becomes an overlooked consideration when hunters select their stand. However, if you are hunting in an area where water is naturally less common, locating a good source of water near a feeding or bedding area, even if it's just a tiny creek, will enhance your chances of seeing deer.

The final interest in a deer's narrow-minded daily living thought process focuses on species continuation. The mating season happens in the fall of the year and is commonly referred to as the rut. Most states' deer hunting seasons coincide with the rutting season. When the rut hits, the well-established survival needs of food and shelter go out the window. The deer are all over each other and will throw common sense to the wind, showing themselves in areas and times of day when they would not normally do so. The rut is a great time to stay in your stand as long as possible, as deer movement is at an all-time high.

Some things you should know about the rut is that the bucks go through a physical transition in which their testosterone levels increase dramatically, resulting in physical changes such as an increase in neck size. Another thing that changes dramatically is their interest in girls, and by this I mean not just one girl but as many does as possible. The does themselves will come into a mating phase known as their estrus cycle. During this cycle, the does will be pretty interested in the bucks as well. The rut is one of the most entertaining and most effective times to be in the woods. If it is only bucks you are after on your bow hunt, you will want to focus your search on finding the does, as the bucks will not be far behind. During the rut, any time a doe is in your area, stay on high alert as a buck is likely to be close by.

Deer Sign – Tracks, Rubs, and Scrapes, not Horoscopes

Once you have located the sustenance and sanctuary locations of your given hunting area, now is the time to look for actual deer sign, clear indications that deer are frequenting the area.

Deer tracks are the most telltale sign that deer are using the area you intend to hunt. The unmistakable hoof print of a deer is unlike that of any other creature that roams its shared woodland habitat. For the most part, the larger the hoof print, the larger the deer. Heavy bodied deer will leave a print that has a wider separation between hoof lobes and can also leave the impression of their dewclaws as part of the larger hoof print. Soft soil will exaggerate the size of any deer and will commonly capture the dewclaws in the print.

It is very difficult to determine the sex of a deer from the hoof print alone. There are theories that bucks tend to drag their feet, leaving drag marks that follow their tracks in shallow snow. There is also the belief that bucks are heavier in the shoulder region (front) while does are heavier in the hip region (rear) and thus a larger front hoof print is that of a buck and a larger rear hoof print belongs to a doe. There are only a select few people who have the ability to consistently and accurately determine deer gender by hoof print alone. They have done so by spending countless hours in the woods and closely analyzing thousands of tracks. If you are spending that kind of time in the woods, you will have no problem finding plenty of deer to hunt.

The two other primary signs to look for are made only by the male of the species. They are commonly referred to as scrapes and buck rubs, and they typically appear very near to each other.

Buck rubs will be found on the base of smaller trees where the rubbing of a deer's antlers has shredded away the bark and revealed a bright spot of exposed wood. Buck rubs begin to show

Buck rubs are saplings, brush, or trees that have been rubbed by a buck's antlers, which shred the bark and reveal bright wood underneath. Fresh buck rubs will stand out amongst the dark trees like a beacon in the woods. Rubs will begin to appear in early September as velvet dries and will increase in number at the approach of the rut.

up as antlers complete their hardening process and the velvet begins to peel away from the antler. Bucks will rub their antlers on trees to remove the velvet and polish their antlers. This is also considered by other bucks to be a territorial marking. As the rut comes into full swing, the number of buck rubs increases dramatically, in line with their aggressive nature, and the trees are looked upon as harmless sparring partners, perhaps in preparation for doing battle with other bucks in the area.

In general, the bigger the rub, the bigger the buck that made it. However, you will be surprised at what a thrashing a young buck can give a small sapling, looking as if a much larger buck had been in the area.

Buck rubs often appear in a line along a deer trail. As the buck travels down the trail, he tangles with a number of small trees, leaving a distinct trail of rubs. This is a good indicator that a buck is in the area, but it does not necessarily mean that several bucks are living there.

Buck rubs are an indicator that you have deer in your area, but they can be misleading, as the newly exposed wood will stay bright for some time. You can determine the freshness of a rub by taking a close look at it (don't touch it as you will leave your scent there) and the ground around it. The shredded bark on a fresh rub will still appear green on its underside and the exposed wood will appear to be moist. If there is a buck standing next to the tree with fresh bark shavings in his antlers, this is a super fresh rub and now you know there is definitely one in the area. But you most likely will not see this (and I am just kidding you a bit here).

Scrapes are perhaps the best indicator of an active buck in your area. Scrapes are normally round circles of pawed earth that occur on or very near a deer trail. They range in size from twelve to thirty-six inches in diameter and are almost always made underneath a low overhanging branch that allows the deer to tangle these with his antlers.

There are several theories regarding the use of scrapes, most commonly that a buck will return to the scrape to see if a doe who is interested in mating has left her scent in the scrape. If so, the buck will follow the does' track until he catches up with her.

Scrapes are very conspicuous in the fall of the year as the leaf-covered ground will have an exposed patch of earth, oftentimes with fresh dirt aggressively flung on top of the leaves around the scrape. Much like buck rubs, it is very common to find more than one scrape in an area.

If you have fresh tracks, scrapes, and buck rubs in your hunting locale, you stand a pretty good chance of having a good hunting opportunity with proper stand set-up and a good offensive game plan to challenge the deer's natural defenses.

Scrapes appear as a clearing on the ground where a buck has aggressively scraped clear any woodland debris and has left his scent as a mating communication to other deer. A scrape is almost always made below a low, overhanging branch in which a buck rubs his antlers or licks the branches.

Choosing a Stand Location

The biggest thing to keep in mind when selecting a location for your hunting stand (they should be called sits), is that you are in the deers' home and they will notice and alter their paths if you destroy the woods in the process of putting up your stand. In other words, keep modifications to a minimum.

Think of it in these terms: if someone changed something in your house, you would notice it. If someone changed something in your house two months ago, you would have accepted it as normal and gotten used to it. Deer are the same way.

You should also think about predominate wind direction and set your stand downwind of where you think you will have a shot at your deer.

If setting up your stands in the summer months, which is preferred, think about what the woods will look like when the leaves have fallen from the trees. Will your stand be exposed like a sore thumb or will it still be well concealed?

Large conifers make great stands, as they have no leaves to lose and will be exactly the same in the fall as they appeared in the summer. Oaks and beech trees have a tendency to hold onto their leaves longer into the fall and also make good trees for stand selection.

Select a solid healthy tree that is within your personal EFFECTIVE KILL RANGE of where you think you will have a shot. Measure the distance from the tree to your shot area and make sure you are efficient at that range.

Deer like edges. The edge of a field, woodlot, tree, or fence line is where deer like to travel. They also prefer to travel just below the crest of a hill rather than on top of it. Think about the path you would have to travel through the area you are hunting to minimize your chances of being seen, because this is what the deer are thinking. Thinking like a deer will help you find your spot.

When setting up your stands, trim only the branches that are necessary to safely access your stand, set your stand to the tree, and shoot without branch or limb interference. Remember, you can only shoot the deer that are right in front of you, so you do not need to clear out a window all the way around the tree.

Make sure the shooting lane to your intended shot area is clear of any branches and trim them well ahead of the season. It takes only a tiny branch extending off a tiny limb to send your arrow off its mark. Also, make sure the shooting lane allows enough room for your bow to be drawn and released when aiming downward towards the ground. Many shooting lanes are generous enough for clear arrow passage, but if the limb next to the stand goes unnoticed until the shot sends the bow into the tree, your bow as well as your dreams of hitting your target may be shattered.

Exercise extreme caution when setting up your tree stand, following the directions to the letter that came with the stand, and be sure to wear your full body harness and lineman's strap while you are setting up your stand. Remember to attach the tree strap for your full body harness to the tree so that it is just about taut when you are seated in your tree stand.

Attach the haul line to your blind, two haul lines if you will be bringing a backpack to your stand with you. The haul lines should be set so that they hang four feet above the ground. By setting your haul lines this way, you will avoid the risk of your gear latching onto debris (branches or roots), making it difficult or impossible to haul it up to your stand. Make sure you have a clear path up the tree for your haul line so your bow or backpack does not get caught on a branch during its ascent or descent.

Measure the distance from your tree stand to the expected area of shot opportunity or other trees surrounding your blind. Make a mental note of the distance to each one so that when a deer is in the area, you will know how far you are from your target and thus how to aim your bow.

Since you will have to travel to and from your blind in the dark, clearly mark a trail leading into your blind for night travel. Reflective push pins can be stuck into the sides of trees to provide a good path in low light conditions without advertising to the world where your stand is located during daylight hours.

Tree Stand for Two, Please

Most likely, your initial bow hunt will happen side by side with your hunting mentor, and man does it rock when you can share your inaugural bow hunting experience. To accommodate two hunters, you can set up a two-man ladder stand, set up two single ladder stands, set up two hang-on stands, or set up one single ladder stand and one single hang-on stand.

The advantage of setting up a two-man stand is that one giant ladder stand holds both hunters. The disadvantages are that a two-man stand is very heavy and thus difficult to set up and that, because of its size, it requires a formidable tree with lots of cover to disguise its presence.

You could locate two trees right next to each other and set up an individual ladder stand in each tree. Single ladder stands are much lighter than two-man stands and offer the great safety feature of easy access by simply climbing the ladder to your seat.

The two-man tree stand, while great for providing a comfortable side-by-side hunting condo for two, is very heavy and thus limits your mobility in the woods.

The Double Hangy is the use of two hang-on stands together to create an awesome dual hunter set-up. This type of blind provides the mentor in the higher blind a bird's-eye view of the other hunter and of the game, as well as great photo or video opportunities. Note: do not set stands directly above one another.

The Ladder/Hangy Combo is the use of a single ladder stand and hang-on stand together. The hang-on stand is set above the ladder stand on the opposite side of the shooting lane. This provides safe, easy access for the youth hunter and a great management view for the mentor.

The use of two hang-on stands together or one hang-on stand with a ladder stand provides a very unique advantage in that you can set the stands so that your mentor is in a stand higher than yours, with a view that looks down past you to your shooting lane. This perspective will provide the mentor with a tremendous camera angle to photograph or videotape the hunt.

Ground Blind

If you have found a great area that does not have any mature trees that will support a tree stand, then the ground blind is your natural alternative. Since you will be at eye level of the deer, concealment of your stand is vital to your success. A ground blind should be made as early as possible to allow the deer to adapt to the change. Take advantage of large brush or tree falls to hide your stand. Make sure you have an open shooting lane to the area where you think your shot will be, measure that distance, and make sure you are efficient at that range.

A pit blind is another stealthy way to make the ground and its landscape work for you. Dig a shallow pit, no more than knee deep, so that you can sit comfortably on its edge, keeping your torso just above ground level. You could also dig your pit just wide enough to accommodate a small stool or chair inside of it. Use the dirt from the blind to help in your concealment by piling it on the backside of your blind, opposite your intended shooting lane, and covering it with nature's debris such as old leaves, fallen branches, etc.

Ground blinds, while featuring the latest camouflage patterns, still must be discreetly built into the landscape through the use of fallen tree debris. They can provide nice protection from the elements when Mother Nature gets nasty. This ground blind has NOT been discreetly located and despite its camouflage color, it stands out like a sore thumb.

Pit blinds are great alternatives when mature trees are just not available in the area you are hunting. The exposed dirt in this picture is a real sign of change that deer would quickly discover. It should be covered with woodland debris, such as fallen leaves or dead grasses.

Do not leave a raw mound of dirt exposed. Blend in the dirt with the natural landscape around your pit blind. The pit blind cannot be too deep or you will not be able to properly extend your bow arm and shoot out of it. If digging a pit blind, make sure it is well marked for your safety as well as the safety of others who may be hunting in your area.

The Defense System of a Whitetail

By now you have practiced with your bow, located your hunting site, and concealed your stand. There is no stopping you now. The only thing that can get in the way of your success is the deer's natural defenses, which are indeed a force to be reckoned with. A deer's primary defense mechanism allows it to know about danger before danger knows about the deer. When you are hunting, you are the danger and they will pick up on you by calling upon their razor sharp senses.

"Smell No Hunter, See No Hunter, Hear No Hunter"

The three defensive barricades you need to overcome to get within bow range of a deer are its phenomenal sense of smell, extremely sensitive hearing, and incredibly perceptive eyesight. Fool all three of these and you have yourself a chance at an archery hunted whitetail, but this is no small feat.

While there are theories on some deer abilities or behaviors, there is a unanimous belief in the hunting world that the sense of smell is the deer's number one defense mechanism. No matter how much camo you have on, if you stink, your chances are minimal, and to deer, human beings stink on ice.

Your body, from head to toe, and everything that you bring into the woods, must be odor free or you are wasting your time. You can exercise all the scent-free practices in the world regarding your own person, but if you are packing your hunting supplies in a school backpack that reeks of cologne or the school itself, you still have an odor problem.

To deer, we are people skunks. Let us suppose for a moment that skunks are vicious man-eaters and prefer to eat kids in the pre-teen to early teenage years. Now, if you smelled one in the woods, you would be gone in a heartbeat, headed for safety. Even after this particular man-eating skunk had left the area, its scent would linger for some time and you still would not feel safe, so you would avoid that area. That is the exact effect we have on deer, so keep your stink down.

In order to be as scent-free as possible, wash your hunting clothes in scent-free detergent and seal them in a plastic bag or container. Bring your exterior hunting clothes to the woods with you and put them on once you have arrived at your hunting destination. Do not wear your exterior hunting clothes around the house, in the car, or at dining spots along the way. Clothes are odor sponges. Hunting boots should be treated the same way.

Take a shower with scent-free soap and use a scent-free deodorant. If you can smell yourself, the deer will be holding their noses at your approach.

At the woods, once you are dressed and ready to go, give yourself and all your equipment a good dousing of scent-eliminating spray. Once you have done all that you can to eliminate your scent, you should enter the woods with the utmost confidence that your smell will not give you away. Just try not to fart while out on your hunt or you will have blown (literally) all of your scent-free work!

Visually, deer have the uncanny ability to pick up on any movement or anything else that is out of place in their surroundings. This means do not move when you are hunting. No scratching. No bug swatting. No fidgeting. It's a lot tougher than it sounds, but it is key to your success. Look around with your eyes by moving them from side to side and using your peripheral vision as much as possible. If you must move, do so very slowly, as quick movements are more apt to draw the attention of a deer. As hard as it is, don't twist yourself around in your stand to see what made that twig snap behind you. You cannot shoot there. Patiently remain at the ready and wait for the deer to come to you.

Now, you do have to move in order to fire your bow, so timing is everything. So many hunters succeed at having deer come within shooting range and then get caught on the draw. Knowing when to draw should be easy for kids. Just pretend your parents are around and you do not want to be seen slugging your sibling. It is that kind of thought process that you need. Just make sure none of the deer in the area are looking at you before you make your move.

Wait for the intended deer to put its head down or look away from you and then be quick and deliberate in your draw. If a deer is moving, its ability to pick you up visually does not seem to be as strong, but do not shoot at a moving deer. Wait until the deer is within your EFFECTIVE KILL RANGE and gives you an opportunity to pull back before you draw your bow. Just about every seasoned bow hunter has a story about drawing on a deer that decided to stop and rest before entering the effective kill range and eventually they could not hold the bow back any longer and spooked the deer before they could get off a shot.

Last but not least, as you have heard one million times from your parents and teachers, be quiet. Total silence is the goal. No tapping your feet on the blind. No iPods ever. Cell phones on silent. No noisy equipment. No blowing bubbles with your gum. No noisy nylon exterior clothing. If you hear any noise at all when you are drawing your bow during your practice sessions, take care of it prior to going out hunting. Listen closely to the wheels or cams of the bow and most importantly to the arrow as it slides its way back across your arrow rest. Look at your bow window and affix pieces of felt anywhere the arrow could come in contact with your bow. Fix the problems before you go hunting or you may squeak away the chance of a lifetime.

An untimely sneeze or cough can literally blow your hunt. If you feel a sneeze coming on, firmly press a finger on the top of your upper lip, where it meets your nose. This will stop a sneeze dead in its tracks. If you feel a cough coming on, try to swallow as much as possible to keep your throat moist. If either is not stoppable, try to sneeze or cough into the sleeve of your jacket as quietly as possible. Hard candies can help keep your throat moist while you are hunting, but unwrap them while they are in your pocket to hold down the noise of the wrapper.

If you can quietly enter the deer woods as an odor-free hunter who can remain statue still while hunting, the deer's odds of survival in your midst have just taken a big step back.

Calling All Deer – Come in, Please

Deer calls come in many shapes and sizes but they all do one thing: when used properly, they can bring elusive deer within range of your stand.

Deer speak a language all their own. It is not filled with slang or text abbreviations but with grunts, bleats, and snorts. There are numerous deer calls available to hunters that will let you have a conversation with the deer you are hunting, but each sound means something different and should be used at different times of the season. There are mouth-activated calls that create sound when you inhale or exhale, depending on the call. In cold climates the inhale calls are more reliable, as exhale calls can freeze once moisture from your breath has accumulated within the call. There are also very effective "can calls" that provide great imitations of doe speak. Say the right thing at the right time and the deer will come right in to your effective kill range, allowing you to bring the conversation to a close.

The words written in this book cannot make the sounds you need to hear to know how to call a deer. Listen to deer when you are in the woods, watch videos specifically on calling deer, or hit the internet for clips of deer sounds. Learn how to speak the language and incorporate deer calling into your archery hunting. The feeling you get when a deer responds to your call is worth all the effort you make to get into the woods.

Making Sense of Deer Scents for the Least Amount of Cents

The deer hunting industry is filled with a variety of scents from a vast array of deer scent companies. Some companies claim to have fresh scent directly from the deer themselves, while others' scents are so fresh they have to be refrigerated when not in use, and still other types of scent cover your scent to make you not so distasteful to a deer's sense.

There are scents for different times of the deer season including pre-rut, rut, and post-rut. Since deer have such sensitive noses and decipher so much of the world around them based on what they smell, the proper use of scents can be a very effective tool to have in your archery arsenal.

Deer scent comes in small bottles as it is very intense in its smell. Be careful to avoid spilling it on yourself and do not open it in the house or in a vehicle as a spill would just plain stink!

During your hunting experience, there will be times when you see deer walking with their nose to the ground like a bloodhound. They are trailing the scent of another deer or something else that has thoroughly caught their attention. If you use a scent that is dispersed on the ground, you could lead one of these bloodhound deer right to your stand.

Deer will also "check the wind" in the area by holding their noses up in the air and taking deep breaths. This is oftentimes done when they are trying to detect danger in their immediate area. To help cover your scent and to aid as an attractant, deer scent can be applied to "deer wicks," small pieces of absorbent material that can be hung from trees in the area around your blind. The scent will disperse amongst the woods with each passing breeze and should be placed upwind of your blind to help cover your own scent.

Deer calls and deer scents, when properly incorporated into your hunting tactics, can provide a deadly advantage for you while in the deer woods.

Your Odds of Success

Each and every thing you do to properly prepare for deer hunting puts more of the odds in your favor and increases your chance at a successful deer hunt. This could be illustrated as follows:

Practicing to efficiency:	25%
Scouting and stand placement:	25%
Taking care of your personal scent:	20%
Sitting still and quiet:	10%
Proper use of calls and deer scent:	5%
Being confident with a positive attitude:	5%

Your odds at archery hunting success are: 90%

The deer's chance at survival when you have done all the right things: 10%

(They are in trouble when you enter the woods!)

The scent market is broken down into two categories, cover scent and attractant scent. Cover scent is designed to eliminate or mask the smell of the hunter. Attractant scent is intended to bring your quarry close to you. Scent wicks hold the scent above the ground, allowing it to travel much further as it is carried off by the wind.

When to Hunt

Deer are most active in the hours just after sunrise and just before sunset. This means you should try to reach your stand thirty minutes before light so that you can enter your stand and allow the area to settle down before daylight enters the woods. How long you stay in the stand on your morning hunts is up to you. Commonly, most hunters give it at least three or four hours per sit. As the rut sets in, deer will be active throughout the day and you could have just as good a chance at shooting a deer at noon as you would early in the morning or later in the evening.

During afternoon hunts, you should try to get to your stand at least three hours prior to sunset and remain in your stand right up until dark settles into the woods. Oftentimes, deer will just begin to feel comfortable enough to come out in the open during the closing minutes of the day and will provide you a shot in the waning minutes of your hunt. Many deerless afternoon hunts suddenly take a turn for the positive at the last possible minute. Stay sharp and at the ready as daylight fades. The term "witching hour" is often attached to the peak hunting timeframes. You want to be in your stand during the witching hours.

Walk Softly

Be mindful of the noise you make as you travel to and from your stand. Pick up your feet and lightly roll them back onto the ground. Avoid stepping on downed branches and twigs as much as you can. The closer you are to your stand, the more mindful you should be of your sound. Since deer are very active in low light conditions, most likely deer will be close to your stand as you enter and exit your location. Leave your stand just as quietly to avoid spooking deer from your area.

How to Shoot a Deer, Shot Selection, and When to Draw

The pre-season practice and continual practice throughout the season has made you a very efficient shot with a bow, at least when shooting at a target. Now you just have to confidently apply that same shooting expertise to a real-life hunting situation. It is of utmost importance to hit a deer in the right spot so that the time from arrow entry to expiration is as short as possible. It will help you to draw on deer that come into your stand area, even if you do not intend to shoot that particular deer. By drawing on numerous deer, you will gain confidence in your technique, reduce the potential for buck fever, and become a more effective hunter. When drawing on deer that you do not intend to shoot, keep your finger away from the trigger release.

When it comes time to draw on a deer, you must be sure that they and any other deer that are with them are not looking towards your stand, as they will pick up on your movement and be gone in no time at all. Wait for your intended deer to put its head down, turn its head, or be distracted by one of the other deer before you begin your draw.

A common mistake that even seasoned bow hunters make is to draw on an animal that is on its way to their effective kill range, only to have the animal put on the brakes and stubbornly refuse to move even one inch more. Many hunters will draw on a deer when its body is blocked by cover in hopes that it will continue its course and walk into the open. In both scenarios, deer have an uncanny ability to sense something is just not right and tend to stay put longer than you can hold back your bow. Once your arms start to shake, your goose is cooked and you will have to let down your bow and ultimately scare away your target.

The heart/lung area of the deer is the kill zone, and placement of the arrow in this area will ensure a quick clean kill.

You have done so much to get ready for this point in time, so be patient and do not rush your shot. Wait for the deer to give you a good broadside shot or quartering away shot. Do not settle for a poor shot where the deer is facing you or facing directly away from you. Shooting a deer at this angle will do nothing more than severely injure the deer and make you feel terrible for doing so.

Do not shoot at a deer that is beyond your EFFECTIVE KILL RANGE (EKR). You may have noticed this term mentioned a few times recently. Know your EFFECTIVE KILL RANGE and stay within it. If you are only confident in your shooting ability out to fifteen yards, then do not shoot at a deer that is twenty yards out. Be patient and confidently shoot at the deer within your own personal EKR. This will vary for everyone and will change as you grow in the sport of archery.

The kill zone on a deer is the same for all deer regardless of gender or species. It is the area just up from and behind the front shoulder bone. It is most openly exposed when the deer moves its front foot forward, opening up the entire vital area to your shot. This area is home to the heart and lungs of your prey. Burn the image of this area into your mind and know that it is the only place you want your arrow to go. Now go a step further and pick a specific hair from this area. Focus on it, bring your bow to full draw without taking your eyes off this spot, find your anchor spot, and let her go.

After the Shot

Once you let that arrow fly, remember to hold your bow in place and keep your drawing arm elevated for perfect shot follow-through. Then focus all your attention on the deer, where you last saw it and which way it was going.

Here is the thing about archery hunting: more often than not, deer do not just fall where they are shot. Deer do not know they have just been shot. What they do know is that suddenly something has happened and they are threatened, so they immediately look for the closest heavy cover to escape danger. They get a quick burst of adrenalin and their survival instincts immediately lead them there.

Keep your eye on the deer you have shot until it is out of sight. Listen closely to the sounds of its departure, specifically if its steps come to an abrupt end or if you hear a thrashing in the leaves. Make a mental note of the direction in which the noise came from.

Then, you must wait. With a good shot, a deer will expire in less than a minute. But since you cannot be exactly sure where you hit the deer, wait at least thirty minutes to get out of your stand and at least sixty minutes before you start tracking your deer.

This is a good time to gather your hunting mentor and others from your hunting party to help you recover your deer. They can also help keep your emotions in check during the tracking process.

Once enough time has passed, first head to the area where you shot your deer and try to recover your arrow or look on the ground for evidence of your shot placement.

A good heart-lung shot will typically provide lots of large blood drops at the scene. If your arrow has passed through the deer, which is not uncommon, it may be right there as well. If it passed through the heart-lung area, it will be covered in crimson blood. If it has very dark, almost black blood on it, the arrow most likely passed through the liver, and if it has bright frothy blood on it, this should be a lung only shot. Any of these shots should yield a recently demised deer at the end of your track.

If your arrow has a yellow fluid on it, this indicates a shot through the stomach and is normally accompanied by a strong smell like that of puke. In the case of a gut shot deer, significant additional time should be allowed before tracking that deer. This will be a fatal shot, but not nearly as quick. You should allow at least eight to twelve hours before tracking a gut shot deer.

Tracking Your Deer – Staying on Course

Tracking is a slow process. Even though you are anxious to get your hands on your deer, if not done properly, it may not happen at all. It is now your responsibility to put all efforts forward in the recovery of your deer. Depending on the shot location, the deer may lie within forty yards or be as far away as four hundred yards or more.

Allow the most experienced hunter in the group to lead the tracking process. Once you have divulged all that happened immediately after the shot to the other members of your party, put together a tracking plan with them and then get after your deer.

Quickly change hats from that of hunter to crime scene investigator to look for clues to the trail that will lead to your deer. The primary clue will be a blood trail but can also be deer hair, overturned leaves, broken branches, etc. Do not disturb, remove, or step on any evidence, as you may need to go back to it to determine the direction of the deer's travel. Visibly mark the evidence (toilet paper is good for this) to create a visible path that can help identify the direction of the deer's travel.

Have a member of your hunting party remain at the last sign you have found while the other members continue their search for more sign. If you are at "last sign," don't just stand there; continue to scour the ground with your eyes and remain patient.

If you are in an area with tall vegetation or lots of trees, expand your search for evidence beyond that of the ground. The wound on the deer will be a couple feet off the ground and thus you may find drops of blood on the tops of tall grasses. Blood or hair may also be found on the sides of trees that the escaping deer has brushed in its hasty and weakened departure.

If your party has lost contact with new evidence, have them return to last sign and begin to walk very slow circles around the last sign as injured deer will oftentimes change directions during their escape.

Remain confident throughout the tracking process. Many times a great hit on a deer could still result in very little sign as fat or tissue has plugged the wound hole, preventing blood from escaping or at the very least providing only trace amounts of a blood trail.

Injured deer are going to head for the thickest, nastiest cover in the immediate area or a water source if there is one close by. Look under trees and brush as you track your deer. You will be amazed at how small an area they can get into when trying to escape danger.

Water soothes wounds, so once a deer figures out what has happened, if there is water close by, it may head to it and lie in it to relieve the injury.

A severely injured deer will immediately look for a good place to lie down. If you jump your deer, or in other words, if you push your deer out of a place where it was lying down, the deer is badly hurt but you are tracking it too soon. Mark the area where you last saw the deer run, leave the area, and return an hour later to resume the track.

If you come upon your deer and it has not yet passed, it may take another well-placed shot with your bow to put it down for good. Be sure the deer has passed before you get too close.

This can be done by touching an eye with a long stick. Any flinch at all indicates the deer has not passed. Typically, when a deer passes, its eyes will remain open and its tongue will hang from its mouth. This may not always be the case, so approach each downed deer with extreme caution. A swift kick with a hoof or solid poke with an antler can cause you or the other members of your hunting party a severe injury.

Recovery of the deer is the completion of the hunt. Be vigilant in your attempts to recover your deer or anyone else's deer in your hunting party. Remain confident throughout the tracking process and never give up on a track unless all efforts have been thoroughly exhausted.

Validate Your License Tag

Immediately upon recovery of your deer, it is important that you validate your archery deer license kill tag by making the proper marks on the tag and affixing it to your deer where indicated in the license rulebook. Typically, it is required that you attach your kill tag to the head (antlers or ears). This is a reliable area to tag your deer, as just about anywhere else may result in having the tag torn off when you are dragging the deer from the woods.

Significant fines can be assessed if you are caught with an untagged deer, even if you have your archery deer license on your person. Conservation officers will allow you very little slack on having an untagged deer.

Dealing with Loss

Regardless of how much preparation you put into your hunt, there are so many variables that can negatively affect your shot, resulting in an injured deer but not to the point of death. This is a disheartening experience for any hunter to go through and has driven some hunters from the sport. Don't let that happen to you.

The natural reaction to this experience will be to replay the event over and over and over in your head. Like an athlete watching game films, determine what went wrong, correct it, and know how to overcome it when presented with the next opportunity. Talk with your hunting mentor or other adult hunters and replay the experience with them to get their input as well on how they have dealt with lost game. In short, learn how to defeat mistakes and do not let mistakes defeat you.

Buck Fever Does Not Just Apply to Bucks

You may have heard about hunters getting buck fever. There is no medical prescription to alleviate this debilitating affliction. It can only be overcome by mental strength and positive attitude.

As the moment of truth draws near, some hunters experience an intense emotional rush that can cause immediate shortness of breath, heavy sweating, elevated heart rate, and uncontrollable shaking. This is buck fever and it can just as well happen when shooting a doe.

Hunting a deer with a bow is an immense step in life and it comes with a lot of positive emotion. These emotions just need to be kept in check until the shot is made. The best way to avoid buck fever is to practice drawing back on any deer that comes within your bow range. Be sure to keep your finger away from the trigger release when doing so. This will build a comfort level with the whole process that occurs when you are about to shoot a white-tailed deer.

If it is a buck you are after and one has entered your field of view, immediately stop looking at the antlers and begin to focus on the kill zone. The antlers can be admired for years to come after the kill. The fixation of a hunter's attention on the antlers only adds fuel to the buck fever fire. Just think "kill zone" and count the antler points when he is in your hand.

Field Dressing Your Deer

Once you have taken a deer, whether it is a doe or a buck, the deer must be field dressed. Now then, this has nothing to do with putting any type of clothing or cool outfits on the deer. Field dressing is the process of removing the entrails from the game animal. Perhaps a more appropriate term would be field undressing, as we are removing the gut inventory from the animal's insides.

This process of field dressing your deer, which is also commonly referred to as "gutting" a deer, does not need to be a bloody scene right out of B grade horror movie. The process is relatively simple and quite frankly proves to be extremely educational, as you get to see the placement of the deer's internal organs and obtain a better understanding as to how their internal operating system works.

Required Tools for Field Dressing

1. One very sharp knife with a sturdy blade (no longer than three and a half to four inches in length).

The most important tool for the field dressing operation is a strong and very sharp knife. A dull knife makes this task much harder and much less safe. When you use a dull knife for any cutting activity, you must apply significantly greater pressure on the blade to get the job done. If you couple this with cold hands and moisture on the handle of the knife, which is highly likely when gutting a deer, the opportunity to slip with the knife increases dramatically, as does the likelihood of a very painful and perhaps serious accident in the field. This can be avoided by always making sure your knife is razor sharp and field ready. A great habit to get into is to always sharpen your knife when you return to camp and are in the process of cleaning it from its use afield. This practice will ensure that your primary cleaning tool is always at the ready.

The size of the knife is also key to efficiently and safely field dressing your deer. You need not have a giant bowie knife or something that resembles a small machete with you. The deer is already dead. You are not hunting the deer with the knife. If you think about it this way, you are actually about to perform a surgical operation and thus would prefer something closer to a scalpel than a meat clever for the job.

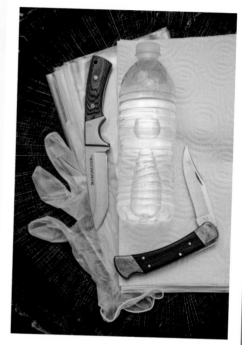

Your field dressing kit, which you have confidently packed in your backpack, should include a knife, surgical gloves, paper towels, re-sealable bags, and water. If you are using your field dressing kit, congratulations!

I find the ideal blade length to not exceed four inches with the blade design itself being somewhat narrow so that you can maneuver the blade (twist it in tight spots) while cleaning the deer. The blade should be rigid and not flexible, like a filet knife used for cleaning fish.

I personally prefer a somewhat beefy handle to help maintain a solid grip while gutting the deer. The larger handle will also provide greater leverage for you when you need to cut through a tougher portion of the deer's body.

Hunting knives come in all shapes and sizes with fixed blades or folding blades, both of which are fine for the job. If you decide to use a folding blade, make sure the folding blade locks into position. This will be much safer when cleaning the deer as the blade will not accidentally fold down upon your fingers. The key to any knife you choose it to keep it sharp and ready to go at all times.

2. **Surgical gloves.**

Using gloves is a good practice to get into. It is much more sanitary and keeps your personal clean-up to a minimum once you have completed field dressing your deer. If you are going to use gloves, I strongly recommend the use of tight-fitting rubber surgical gloves as opposed to baggy plastic gloves that are sold at many hunting stores. Surgical gloves can be bought at any medical supply store and most pharmacies. I suggest you include the gloves as part of your essential hunting inventory and keep these with you when afield.

There are two primary advantages of surgical gloves over plastic gloves: feel and grip. The tight-fitting surgical gloves allow you more sensitivity in your fingertips and are much less likely to slip on the knife handle once they become wet.

3. **Two one-gallon size re-sealable plastic bags** (you can use one bag to pack the heart and/or liver or tenderloins and the other to pack out any messy paper towels used in the clean-up process).

4. **Bottled water** to rinse hands and knife upon completion of the gutting process.

5. **Paper towels** to wipe and dry hands.

6. **Old hand towel** for cold weather hand warm-ups.

Archery deer season often coincides with cold weather in many states. When cleaning a deer in cold weather conditions your hands may get cold, and this could be a hazard should your fingertips become numb. You should periodically take a break to warm your hands, but you are not going to want to put your messy hands into your gloves or pockets to do so. Wrapping your hands in an old hand towel and wringing them together will bring the warmth back in just a couple of minutes.

Before You Start

1. Believe it or not, this actually has to be said: make sure the deer is indeed dead before you start the field dressing process. You would be surprised at how many folks have walked up on their deer, assumed it has passed, prepared to clean it, and just before they started, find their deer has come to and escaped, oftentimes never to be seen again.

2. If the deer has passed in heavy cover, move the deer to a nearby open spot. This will make the cleaning process easier for you and allow other members of your hunting party to readily locate and identify you.

3. Have all your cleaning items unpacked and ready for use. By this I mean your plastic bags and water or paper towels. You do not want to find yourself in a situation where your hands are quite messy after cleaning the deer and then you have to rummage through your pack to get to your cleaning items.

4. Clear a space on the ground of any leaves, snow, or debris and place all cleaning items in this one spot. Amongst the excitement of a successful hunt, it is very easy to misplace a piece of equipment, costing you time or replacement money of the missing item.

5. Finally, roll up your sleeves, and if you have a watch, remove it and place it immediately in your pack or in your pocket. Do not place it on the ground, as it may end up spending the rest of its time in that final resting spot.

The Rezmer Technique

Every hunter has his or her own personal routine they like to go through when cleaning their deer. Some are terribly inefficient and just plain messy, which costs the hunters unnecessary time afield and ruins much of the prime meat within the deer.

While researching the best way to instruct new hunters about the process of field dressing, I had the very good fortune to meet Leonard (Lennie) Rezmer, a vice president of Eastman Outdoors, Carbon Express, and Gorilla Treestands. With Lennie comes the most efficient, effective, and safest way to clean a deer I have come across.

I will refer to Lennie's process as the "The Rezmer Technique."

Lennie is an outdoorsman in the truest sense of the word. He is an extremely skilled archer with international hunting experience and a mastery of the technical side of the sport. He is also known for his unbelievable tracking skills. Some folks claim he is part Sioux Indian and part bloodhound, and his recovery rate for finding other hunters' supposed lost game is astonishingly high.

Lennie has himself had tremendous success afield, which has given him reason enough to clean hundreds of animals. But like many other hunters, Lennie is a true sportsman and has shared his knowledge mentoring many young hunters and helping many seasoned hunters recover their deer and assisting in the field dressing of their game. All of this experience has enabled Lennie to develop the very efficient Rezmer Technique, which at his best allows him to completely clean a deer in less than one minute! This is an illustration of his efficiency and should in no way be considered a challenge to you to speed gut your deer. Take your time, be careful, and do not rush the process. This is a tremendous opportunity for you to learn the internal operating system of the white-tailed deer.

Step 1:

The deer must be on its back, belly facing skyward to begin. It will be very helpful if you can drag the deer next to a small tree or sapling. Rest the deer up against the tree, with the belly facing upward, and wrap the front leg closest to the tree, around the tree. This will support the deer in the belly-up position and keep at least one leg from swinging into you as you field dress the deer. If you have someone with you, the best assistance they can provide is to hold the front legs of the deer steady and apart as you go through this process.

Please note: when making the external cuts into the deer, only insert the blade of the knife deep enough into the deer to cut the skin. Throughout the field dressing process, it is essential that you avoid cutting the intestinal tract, urinary tract, and stomach as the fluids from any of these can seep into the meat and adversely affect the flavor. The best way to avoid this is to not penetrate the entire knife blade into the deer but only go deep enough to do the necessary work in the initial field dressing steps.

It is also imperative that you make sure the arrow and the broadhead are no longer in the body of the deer. If you have not recovered both the entirety of the arrow and the broadhead, most likely part of either has remained within the deer and you need to proceed through the entire field dressing process with extreme caution. If you locate either item within the deer, safely remove them before continuing your work.

Step 2: DOES ONLY, *Removal of Milk Sac*

a. Remove the milk sac at the rear underbelly of the deer by grabbing hold of the milk sac and slightly pulling upward on the sac.

b. Make a slit at the front of the sac and follow around to the back of the deer on each side of the milk sac.

c. The cuts on each side should meet up at the rear of the deer and then you can pull off the milk sac.

DOES ONLY, *Removal of Colon and Vaginal Area*

a. Make a deep cut all the way around the anus and vagina of the deer. For this cut, you can sink the extent of the knife blade into the deer to cut all muscle tissues attached to this area. You want to cut around both rather than through them. Once you complete this circular cut, do not attempt to pull this tissue out. It will pull out with the rest of the entrails when they are removed.

Step 2: BUCKS ONLY, *Removal of Colon and Genitals*

a. Grab hold of the deer's genitals and carefully cut around the entire genital area, being careful not to cut the urinary tract.

b. Once the external cut has been made around the genitals, pull them from the deer, cutting any attached membrane tissue. Discard the genitals.

c. Move to the anus of the deer and again insert the entire length of the blade next to the anus and cut all the way around the anus. This will pull out with the rest of the entrails when they are removed.

Step 3:

a. Once the sexual organs and anus have been taken care of, cut down to the pelvic bone and run your knife blade along the entirety of the pelvic bone, allowing the rear legs to separate even further.

Step 4:

a. Return to the cut at the rear of the belly, where we removed either the milk sac or the genitals. This is where the pelvic bone meets the stomach of the deer.

b. Make a vertical slit approximately two inches long in this area.

Step 5:

a. Take your free hand and place your index finger and middle finger into the slit. Spread open your fingers while pulling upward on the skin.

b. In your knife hand, place the blade so that the handle sits across your life line in your palm and the top of the blade is setting on your index finger, slightly protruding past the tip of your index finger.

c. With the blade facing upwards, carefully place the knife tip between your two fingers that are pulling up on the belly skin of the deer and run the knife tip up to the brisket of the deer.

Step 6A: If NOT Shoulder Mounting Your Deer

a. If you are not going to shoulder mount the deer, pull your free hand away from the deer and place both hands firmly on the handle of the knife. Apply strong pressure and continue cutting upward through the brisket of the deer until you come in contact with the base of the neck.

Step 6B: If Shoulder Mounting Your Deer

a. Make sure your sleeves are pulled up very high, and keeping the knife in hand, enter both hands into the chest cavity of the deer, pushing them underneath the brisket up towards the neck of the deer.
Be very careful as this is a blind surgical procedure. Grab hold of the windpipe and esophagus, which will feel like two large tubes running out of the deer's neck, and cut entirely through each at the base of the neck.

b. Remove both hands and set the knife aside.

c. If shoulder mounting your deer, you do not need to perform step 8.

Step 7:

a. Pulling the chest cavity open, you will see the diaphragm, which is a tough, thin muscle that separates the heart/lung area from the stomach area. Cut the diaphragm away from the rib cage on each side of the deer.

Step 8:

a. Enter the knife at the top of the chest cavity opening, at the base of the neck, and cut through the windpipe and esophagus.

   b. Remove both hands and set the knife aside.

Step 9:

a. Place both hands on the entrails at the top of the neck and firmly pull all the entrails down through the rear legs of the deer.

b. At this point, you can reach into the rear of the body cavity and pull the anus free through the inside and continue to pull it out of the body cavity with the rest of the entrails.

All of the guts should be free from the body of the deer and you have just completed your first official field dressing. Congratulations!

If you will be consuming the heart and/or liver, locate each within the gut pile and carefully remove them, placing them in the plastic bag you brought with you as part of your field essentials. The tenderloins (2), are located alongside the spine, where the ribs attach. These can be removed in the field or once you return to camp. The tenderloins are considered to be the best cut of meat that your deer has to offer. Be cautious and thorough in your removal of such so that no meat is wasted in the process.

Once all the entrails have been removed from the deer, there may be a pool of blood at the bottom of the chest cavity. Roll the deer over so that the blood drains from the cavity.

Post Field Dressing Clean-Up

Once all the work is complete, make sure you recover any items you may have placed on the ground during the field dressing process. Be sure to pack out any paper towels, rubber gloves, or water bottles you used to clean the deer.

Now that you have removed your garbage, nature will send in her own garbage men to take care of the gut pile. In the great circle of life, the organs you are leaving behind will soon be a well-appreciated meal for coyotes, raccoons, turkey vultures, crows, and any other scavengers in the area. It is not uncommon to return to the scene of the crime the very next day and find all the evidence has been removed. Nature's scavengers are very meticulous so as to not waste any bit of the meal you have left for them.

Whatta Drag!

Dragging a deer out of the woods is a real butt kicker. The level of difficulty varies tremendously based on the size of the deer, the ruggedness of the terrain, and the distance you must travel. This is an effort that is best done with more than one person. Do not rush the task and take several breaks while dragging your deer, especially if you are dragging your deer with someone of advanced age or in poor physical health.

To make the drag a little easier, tie up the front legs of the deer behind its head. Then tie a short rope (maybe twelve inches in length) from the head of the deer onto the middle of a sturdy stick (maybe thirty-six inches in length). The stick will act as a well-balanced handle for two draggers to work together in pulling the deer from the woods. This method will lift the deer's head and front feet off the ground, reducing drag and limiting its ability to snag up on small saplings and other ground obstructions. Truly take the road of least resistance (the most direct route) when dragging a whitetail from the autumn woods.

There are several tools that can help make a drag much easier, the best being motorized tools such as a four-wheeler or other ATV. But in the absence of motorized vehicles, heavy duty plastic sleds or wheeled deer carts will significantly reduce the amount of energy that is expended in removing your deer from the woods.

Hanging the Deer

Once the deer has made it back to camp, I find it best to hang it from its head or neck. On a mature tree, locate a solid limb approximately ten feet off the ground and throw a rope over the limb. Tie the rope around the neck or at the base of the antlers and pull the deer up so that the rear legs are hanging above the ground. If you are in an area where coyote, fox, or raccoons are prevalent, make sure the deer hangs at least three feet off the ground to avoid these predators coming in for a midnight snack on the lower extremities of the deer.

I prefer the head's up method of hanging a deer, as this allows any remaining fluids to drain from the deer and not gather at the neck of the deer, slowly absorbing into the meat.

If sunny or lukewarm conditions prevail, make sure to hang the deer in a well shaded area.

The only thing left inside the body cavity of the deer that will cause further damage to the meat is blood. If blood is allowed to absorb into the meat, it will make for a less than pleasing flavor. To avoid this, wash the inside of the cavity with cool water until all blood and blood clots are rinsed free from the inside.

It is key to cool the inside of the body cavity, and the best way to do this is to place three to four short sticks inside the chest cavity to hold the cavity open. This will allow air to flow freely through the cavity and cool the meat.

If temperatures will be hovering above forty degrees for the majority of the day, I strongly suggest processing the deer at once or taking it to a processor to remove and package the meat.

In early bow season, conditions often exist that are warm enough to invite flies to your freshly killed deer. To avoid their contact with your deer, you can generously sprinkle black pepper within the cavity of the deer. You can also wrap the deer in cheesecloth, which will keep the flies out but still allow air to flow through the deer.

Whitetail Facts

The whitetail is a truly amazing animal with equally amazing abilities that enable it to survive in all types of harsh weather conditions and unfriendly terrains. It is highly adaptable with a population that has flourished despite pressures on the herd incurred by the expansion of humans and urban sprawl.

John Ozoga, a former Department of Natural Resources Wildlife Research Biologist at the Cusino Wildlife Research Station, has authored or co-authored about one hundred technical research articles, seven popular books on white-tailed deer, and hundreds of magazine and newspaper articles. John is currently the research editor for Deer & Deer Hunting magazine and writes a whitetail column for Michigan Out-of-Doors magazine.

Following are some of the more interesting facts Mr. Ozoga has learned during his time with the white-tailed deer:

1. There are thirty-eight subspecies of white-tailed deer, thirty of which are located in North and Central America.

2. The species *cervidae* (deer) grows antlers that are the only growing appendage in the animal kingdom; their temperature is equal to the body's core, actually being warm to the touch.

3. Antlers are the only mammalian appendage that replaces itself annually.

4. Antlers experience peak growth in May and June with most development completed by late July or early August. The antler hardening process actually starts early in the growth process, beginning at the base of the antler. Once fully hardened, the velvet will shed from the antlers and bucks will oftentimes make their initial rubs in an effort to remove the velvet from their antlers.

5. At their peak, moose antlers can grow at the rate of three-quarters of an inch per day, maybe more. Deer antlers probably grow at the rate of one quarter to one half inch per day.

6. Disfigured antlers sometimes develop as the result of body injury, especially broken bones. Oftentimes, a broken leg results in a deformed antler on the opposite side, referred to as "contralateral effects."

7. The photoperiod (shortening of daylight hours) sets off the breeding season for deer so that fawns are born during the best vegetative conditions, allowing them their best chance of survival. This is a much more narrow window of time in the northern regions than it is in southern regions.

8. Whitetail gestation is about two hundred days. In the northern range, most adult does (does that are one and a half years and older) breed in November and give birth in late May or early June. Some doe fawns breed when seven to eight months old, generally in December, and give birth in late June or July.

9. A doe's nutritional intake in the last third of gestation is key to producing a healthy fawn(s).

10. Healthy fawns weigh between seven to eight pounds, maybe more, at birth.

11. Fawns consume sixteen to eighteen ounces of milk a day.

12. Malnourished and younger does, on average, produce more bucks than does. Older and well-nourished does, on average, produce more does than bucks.

13. Does with newborn fawns remain very territorial in the first four to six weeks of a fawn's life.

14. The initial territory in which a doe will keep her fawns is a ten- to twenty-acre range. The fawns learn the boundaries of this area and stay within it if threatened.

15. Does spend the initial four to six hours after birth with their fawns. The doe consumes the afterbirth, sometimes even the stained vegetation, thus minimizing odors that might attract predators. The fawns nurse almost immediately, generally while the mother lies on her side. Colostrum milk, produced by the doe for a short time after giving birth, provides antibodies necessary to resist disease.

16. After the initial birth period, the doe will separate the fawns anywhere from one hundred to four hundred feet away from each other to help keep the entire family safe from predators. Fawns continue to bed separately for eighteen to thirty-two days. This minimizes the risk of both being killed should a predator happen by.

17. Does will move their fawns from their bedding sites (after feeding and a bathroom break) two to three times a day.

18. Newborn whitetails are "hiders," which is their chief defense against predators.

19. The fawns of younger does have a higher mortality rate than fawns of older does as the young does are not as protective (or have not learned to be as yet).

20. Older does are more protective of fawns even against such predators as bears and wolves.

21. Does come into estrus typically two to three times per mating season in the northern range and up to six to seven times in the southern range.

22. Adult deer can consume between one to two tons of food annually.

23. Adult deer can clear fences up to eight feet high when jumping.

24. Northern deer migrate from their summer range to a winter range that can be over fifty miles away. This migration is a learned behavior and the travel route is learned by the young as they follow adult deer to and from each range. This range can be similar for generations of deer, as deer are very traditional in their established range.

25. Albino deer occur in about one in eighteen thousand deer.

26. Piebald deer (deer with large white patches) occur in about one in one thousand deer.

27. Does can grow antlers; this happens as frequently as one in 2,500 does.

28. Does can produce fawns throughout their entire lives and do not incur a non-productive time unless they are malnourished or ill.

29. The oldest recorded deer in captivity reached twenty-three years of age.

30. In the wild, deer have been known to reach nineteen to twenty years of age.

31. While most bucks shot are one and a half years old, this is not the average. The average buck age varies from one area to another, depending upon hunting pressure.

Hunting Friendships and Lifelong Bonds

There is an old saying that you can't choose your family, but you can choose your friends. This is especially true when it comes to hunting, although some of your closest hunting buddies will be your family members. Hunting has a deep personal meaning to those who are truly serious about the sport. To these folks, hunting is a passion and all things that relate to it are near and dear to their hearts.

With hunting comes extreme emotional highs and lows and these will be shared with the folks you have chosen as your hunting buddies. The common sharing of these intense experiences will create a bond that is so much more than a casual friendship. Family-type bonds have been built through the annual traditions of deer hunting and deer camps. Parent/child relationships are also deeper and more meaningful as a result of these shared experiences, as are all other friendships that are built around the sport.

The other basis of hunting friendships is the uninterrupted quiet time that is spent together in long travels, scouting walks, or unified efforts in preparation of hunting sites or food plots. Despite the overall short season that deer hunting claims on a calendar, to you and your hunting buddies, it is a conversation that never fades throughout the year and intensifies as the months toward the next season grow smaller in number. Hunting buddies, much like the sport itself, will be one of your life's greatest riches.

The Need for Hunting and Standing up for Your Rights

Hunting is more than just an outdoor recreational sport, it is a necessity to the survival of the species. That may sound a bit odd, but here is how it plays out in this modern era.

Deer are extremely prolific creatures. In other words, they are very proficient at making a lot more of themselves. Years ago, numerous natural predators fed on deer and kept their populations in line with what the environment in the area could support. Basically, only so much food will support only so many animals.

Along came man who got rid of the dangerous predators, as they were a threat to us as well. Then we began to build cities and suburbs and develop the land the deer once called home. Remember, deer are very good at making more of themselves and are extremely adaptable to changes in their environment. With their natural predators gone, deer had nothing to keep their populations in check and eventually began to exhaust the food supply in their area. Once the food was gone, starvation set in, which is nature's extremely cruel way of controlling population when there is no other means to do it.

In my opinion, the sport of hunting is not only the ultimate outdoor experience for sportsmen, it is a good way to control the population of the deer herd in each state or province. Death by an arrow can take minutes or sometimes just seconds. Death by starvation is a painful death that occurs over months.

The state of Michigan offers a great example of how prolific deer are and how hunting is vital in controlling their population. The average whitetail population in Michigan has hovered around 1.5 million animals over the last several years. In all, the state's deer hunters, both bow and gun combined, harvest approximately 500,000 animals each deer season. Additionally, tens of thousands of deer are killed in car deer accidents around the state. Despite this significant harvesting of deer each year, Michigan's whitetail population remains constant in the range of 1.5 million animals.

If hunting were to disappear, the population of white-tailed deer would quickly overwhelm the food supply wherever deer roam and massive starvation would decimate the herd. Hunting is scientifically necessary for the survival of the species.

Despite the facts, some individuals look down on hunting and all who participate in it. You may have the unfortunate luck to encounter some of these folks in your life. Stand up for your rights as a hunter and defend the sport by trying to educate those who do not understand its necessity.

Uphold the Hunter's Ethical Code

"Ethical behavior is doing the right thing when no one else is watching, even when doing the wrong thing is legal." This was said by one of America's founders of conservation, Aldo Leopold. In summary, whatever you do while you are afield is a reflection on the entire hunting population. Treat other hunters, non-hunters, landowners, and anyone else you come across with the utmost respect. Your actions during these encounters will affect the mindset of the general population towards the hunting population. You must treat animals, private property, and all with whom you share the outdoors with the same level of respect that you expect from others towards you.

Capturing the Moment

Despite days and days of preparation and endless hours spent in the field, hunting adventures are summed up in one click of the camera button. Keep your adventure alive by grabbing it with a photo that will tell the story without words.

Once a hunt has come to an end, even if game was not taken, preserve the memory of the experience with a photo of all in attendance. Make sure everyone is in their hunting outfits with something in the backdrop that is unique to the area in which you were hunting. Even if a deer did not fall on a particular hunt, you still had the adventure of hunting and the anticipation of "what if" that comes from being afield. Appreciate every moment out there and relive those memories as well.

The "trophy shot" as it is so commonly called is the picture of the hunter and the hunted together. The best trophy shots include the others who were along for the adventure and are taken right at the moment the deer was recovered, when emotions are at their all-time high. Position the animal so that the appearance of blood is kept to a minimum and bring your bow into the picture with you. Keep the shot tight so that the hunter and the game are the majority of the picture and are not lost in too much background. There is no need for anyone to say "Smile," as you won't be able to help yourself.

The Bow Hunter's Journal

Now this is looking way down the road for you, but life's greatest riches are the people and the experiences that are a part of your life. The hunting tales from seasons past and the bonds of friendship that grow throughout each one will enrich you far beyond what you will realize in your youth.

A well-kept hunting journal will serve as a vault of invaluable experiences that are protected within its covers. It will help you relive and share the outstanding adventures that occurred during your time afield. The written words can incorporate the small details that led to great success or caused the deer of a lifetime to stop just short of showing himself to you completely.

Add to the journal a couple of encapsulating photos of all who were in attendance during that season's hunt and you have in your hands a vivid recollection of experiences that might otherwise fade with the years between seasons.

Among other things, you might write the following in your journal:

Hunt Date

Hunt Location

Hunting Members

Weather Conditions

Animals Seen

Summary of Hunt

Memories of the Hunt

Bow Hunter's Journal pages are included with this book beginning on page 81.

Final Thoughts

The words within this book are intended to provide you with the knowledge you need to successfully enter the world of archery deer hunting. Much of this information was learned in my time afield, after years of being close to success and painfully learning the many things that can go wrong while in pursuit of the whitetail deer with stick and string. I hope the information between the covers of this book leads you to success in your hunt and steers you to a life full of unforgettable archery adventures. Remember, the gift of the outdoors is truly a gift for life. Shoot Straight!

The Bow Hunter's Checklist

Before you head out on your Archery Adventure, make sure you have all the necessary items below, including a positive mental attitude and confidence in yourself and your archery skills:

Safety Equipment:

Directional:

- [ ] Compass
- [ ] Whistle
- [ ] Flashlight with fresh batteries
- [ ] Walkie talkie
- [ ] GPS
- [ ] Cell phone

Hunting Plan:

- [ ] Did you tell a responsible person who is not hunting with you where you are hunting, what time you should be back, and that you will check in with them upon your return?

Injury:

- [ ] First aid kit
- [ ] Water

Weather:

- [ ] Extra warm layer of clothes
- [ ] Rain jacket or plastic rain parka
- [ ] Hand warmers
- [ ] Emergency safety blanket

Hunting Equipment:

- [ ] Full Body Safety Harness and lineman's belt
- [ ] Bow
- [ ] Arrows
- [ ] Release
- [ ] All camouflage clothes including hat, gloves, jacket, pants, and boots
- [ ] Hunting mask or face paint
- [ ] Scent eliminating spray
- [ ] Backpack for carrying all your necessary gear
- [ ] Length of rope for dragging your deer
- [ ] Field dressing kit including knife, re-sealable bags, paper towels, water
- [ ] Binoculars
- [ ] Camera

The Bow Hunter's Journal

Date _____

I bowhunted at _____

_____

I bowhunted with _____

_____

I saw _____

_____

Deer Harvested _____

_____

Date _____

I bowhunted at _____

_____

I bowhunted with _____

_____

I saw _____

_____

Deer Harvested _____

_____

Date _____

I bowhunted at _____

_____

I bowhunted with _____

_____

I saw _____

_____

Deer Harvested _____

_____

Date _____

I bowhunted at _____

_____

I bowhunted with _____

_____

I saw _____

_____

Deer Harvested _____

_____

The Bow Hunter's Journal

Date _____

I bowhunted at _____

_____

I bowhunted with _____

_____

I saw _____

_____

Deer Harvested _____

_____

Date _____

I bowhunted at _____

_____

I bowhunted with _____

_____

I saw _____

_____

Deer Harvested _____

_____

Date _____

I bowhunted at _____

_____

I bowhunted with _____

_____

I saw _____

_____

Deer Harvested _____

_____

Date _____

I bowhunted at _____

_____

I bowhunted with _____

_____

I saw _____

_____

Deer Harvested _____

_____

The Bow Hunter's Journal

Date _____

I bowhunted at _____

_____

I bowhunted with _____

_____

I saw _____

_____

Deer Harvested _____

_____

Date _____

I bowhunted at _____

_____

I bowhunted with _____

_____

I saw _____

_____

Deer Harvested _____

_____

Date _____

I bowhunted at _____

_____

I bowhunted with _____

_____

I saw _____

_____

Deer Harvested _____

_____

Date _____

I bowhunted at _____

_____

I bowhunted with _____

_____

I saw _____

_____

Deer Harvested _____

_____